PLAY DEAD

J.H. WEAR

For Laura.
A promising life ended by an impaired driver.
A beautiful, young woman we shall never forget.

PRELUDE

Jacob Carlton took a puff from his cigarette, cursing that he had to walk home. He continued his journey, reaching a fence that protected a schoolyard. After climbing over the fence, he crossed the field toward the school. He had considered returning to the bar parking lot where his truck waited but suspected the cops might be watching out for him to do just that. They had shown up at the altercation he was involved in at the bar and once they took his name, he guessed they had checked his records. That meant they would have little patience for any more wrongdoing.

Carlton took a final drag from his smoke and threw it on the ground, stepping on the butt as he went by. Another few blocks and he would reach his apartment, where cold beer and leftover pizza waited in the fridge.

He reached the edge of the schoolyard and began to cut across the nearly empty parking lot. The dark asphalt wasn't close to the streetlights, making it hard to see details.

"Hey, Carlton."

He turned, startled. At first, he didn't see the figure at the edge of the parking lot. "What? Who are you?"

"It's debt payment time."

The first shot, a pop from a handgun with a silencer, dropped him, hitting him in his stomach. He moaned as he lay on his back. "Help me."

The figure walked over to where he lay holding his midsection. The gun was pointed right at his chest.

"No, please." Carlton's jaw quivered as his eyes focused on the gun barrel. Another popping sound and Carlton was dead.

1

Anya Roberts clicked on the keyboard, adding details to a file. Her desk was cluttered with yellow Post-it notes, pads of paper, two cup-sized cylinders holding pens, scissors, a small ruler, highlighters, and a stick holding a small flag of New Zealand. Across from her desk sat Moss Stone, her current detective partner, and previous to that, a man she had slept with. That had been a mistake, she reflected afterward, but what was done, was done. After the initial period of difficult conversation, they settled into a relationship of friendship.

"Moss." She waited a moment and repeated his name, only louder.

"What?" He reluctantly lowered the magazine.

"What's in that magazine that's so interesting? Shouldn't you be working?"

"In a way, I'm working. I'm reading an article on entangled particles."

"How does that possibly relate to doing police work? And suddenly, I regret asking that question."

"Because entangled particles are just another way to show how everything in the universe is connected. If one entangled particle has its properties changed, the other particle immediately changes as well. Now, detective work is largely finding clues. Knowing how things can be interconnected can help solve crimes."

"I knew I shouldn't have asked." She sighed. "Anyway, we need to get some work done that's actually recognized in the department as being work related."

"All right, I guess I can work on some of the case reports."

"Yeah, you doing reports. I'll believe it when I see it."

"Come on..." The desk phone rang. Stone picked it up. "Homicide, Stone speaking." After a short conversation, he hung up. "Good news, we have a murder."

"Your definition of good news is different than most people, obviously." She stood and grabbed her purse.

Stone put on his jacket. "The victim, a male, was found dead in a school parking lot. He has two bullet holes in him."

"Lovely. I'm amazed how you think going to a murder scene is better than doing a report."

"What can I say? I'm not a desk person. Let me grab a coffee, and we can get going."

She shook her head at the thought of another coffee.

————

Yellow tape indicated the perimeter behind which mere civilians were required to stand. Most of those watching were school-aged kids, with a couple of adults trying to keep them from crossing the yellow tape. In the middle of the parking lot, a dark sheet covered most of a body, with a pair of black boots sticking out at the end. A few feet away a dirty white baseball cap rested on the asphalt.

A reporter hurried over to them, guessing they looked like the authorities investigating the murder scene. "Pat Pisesky, CHED news. Can you tell us anything?"

Stone held up his hand. "Sorry, we just arrived. No info yet."

Roberts and Stone entered past the yellow tape and approached the officer who appeared to be in charge.

After introductions, Stone asked, "What can you tell us?"

The cop flipped open his notebook, reading. "According to the ID he had in his wallet, the body is Jacob Carlton. The wallet still had cash in it. The other items of note are keys and a cell phone. The apparent cause of death was two gunshot wounds, one in the stomach and the second in the chest. No witnesses have come forward." He shrugged, giving the impression he wasn't surprised at the lack of witnesses. "I have his address, or at least the one on his driver's licence."

"Okay, thanks." Stone walked over to the body and lifted up the sheet covering it. The grey shirt had two large bloodstained spots that joined together in a gruesome figure eight. Stone glanced at the pale face. A mop of hair needing a cut suited the unshaven face.

"Anything?" Roberts inquired.

Stone replied in an even voice, "Blood on his shirt indicates he wasn't standing long when he was shot. The blood was spread evenly around. It didn't have time to soak downward. I guess that doesn't mean much, other than whoever shot him likely put the second shot in when he was already lying down. They didn't take his wallet, so this wasn't a robbery. Someone wanted him dead for who he was. Judging by his looks, I suspect it wasn't a jilted girlfriend."

The cop who gave him the earlier details returned holding his notebook.

"I just received some more information about the victim. He was in a bar fight earlier in the evening. According to the report, he was in one of two groups that had a few words and later a pushing match when they were ejected from the bar. That was at ten twenty-two last night. Carlton was told by the responding police he wasn't allowed to drive home because of his apparent level of intoxication." The cop closed his notebook. "The bar is called the Dragonhead's and it's about four blocks from here. It could be the fight didn't end at the bar."

"Sounds like a possibility." Stone frowned. "When the examiner's office has paid a visit, get the body out of here. We don't need this to be a classroom topic in show-and-tell."

Roberts scribbled in her notebook. "Carlton doesn't live far from here. I suggest we knock on a few doors around here to see if anyone heard or saw anything. Then, we go to his home address. If he lives with anyone, we'll have some unhappy news to deliver."

Stone grunted, acknowledging that was the most unpleasant part of any homicide investigation, notifying the next of kin of a death.

They returned to the yellow tapeline, and again, the reporter stepped in front of them. "What can you tell me about what happened?"

Stone sighed. "Just that a male in his late twenties has been found dead in the parking lot. His death is being investigated as a homicide."

"Any names?" The male reporter sounded eager.

"Sorry, not until we talk to the next of kin and maybe not even then." Stone knew the press sometimes were irritated by the police's refusal to release the names of victims. The police chief claimed even when dead, a person's privacy had to be protected.

Roberts and Stone crossed the street, ringing the doorbell of a bungalow with pale blue siding hiding part of dull-coloured stucco. The occupant, an elderly man, dressed in a sweater despite the warm temperature, opened the door halfway.

Stone held up his badge, and the man peered at it. "What's this all about?"

"There has been a murder across the street in the parking lot." Stone pointed at the scene of the crime. "Did you hear anything unusual last night?"

"No. We go to bed early and ignore all the shenanigans going around that darn school." He began to push the door closed but stopped long enough to add his worldly opinion. "Not surprised about another killing. Ever since that idiot Trudeau got elected things have been going to hell in a handbasket." He shut the door.

Stone raised his eyebrows and looked at Roberts. "Now, I do believe everything is connected, but how does electing a government put a bullet in someone?"

"It's a stretch. Let's hope the next house is less politically biased."

The following house was a mirror image of the first, although the exterior had been completely redone with white siding covering the front. A woman in her thirties answered the door, giving them a tired smile when they showed their identification.

"Is this about what happened across the street?"

"Yes." Stone repeated his question if she heard anything.

"Not really. The usual traffic noises. This is a school area but vehicles feel free to speed around here. Someone in the neighbourhood has a car that makes a lot of noise and I hear it every night. Other than that, I guess I tune out the traffic noise."

"So, nothing different?" Roberts asked.

The woman pursed her lips as she looked up. "Hmm. I heard a bike. Not the big kind, but one of those fast, smaller bikes. I think it went up and down the street, and then, it was gone. I tell you it's hard getting the kids to go to sleep in the summer with all that noise sometimes."

They thanked her and went to the third house. A teenaged girl answered the door, looking bored.

"Yeah?"

Roberts showed her identification. "We're investigating a crime scene across the street. Are your parents' home?"

"Nope. They went out." She continued with her disinterested stare.

"Did you happen to see or hear anything last night?"

She gave a cheeky smile. "Not here. I went out last night."

"What time did you come home?"

"What business is it of yours?"

"Our business is in investigating a murder. If you were out last night, did you see anything in the parking lot across the street when you came home?"

The girl finally took a closer look across the street. Her jaw dropped slightly. "Oh. I came home at nine thirty or so. My curfew is ten. I didn't see anything."

Roberts passed over her business card. "Please have your parents contact us if they saw or heard anything at all unusual last night."

"Okay." The girl studied the card. The bored look had disappeared.

The next house, a two-story home, looked new. Stone speculated the original house had been torn down and replaced by the taller structure.

The man answering the door was polite, inviting them inside.

"Charles Gault." He said in the way of an introduction as he led them to the living room. "Coffee? Tea?"

Stone declined the offer. "We're just asking if you, or anyone in the household, heard anything last night. There was a murder committed in the school parking lot."

Gault was silent for a moment. "That's awful to hear something like that happened so close to our home. No, I can't say I heard anything different last night. We, my family and I, were downstairs watching TV and sound doesn't travel very well down there."

"So, no traffic noise? No gunshot sounds?"

Gault cocked his head. "No gunshots, but I did hear a motorbike. That's a bit unusual here as there aren't many bike owners on this street."

"Do you recall what time you heard that?"

He smiled. "Yes, as a matter of fact, I do. The TV show we were watching ended at eleven. So I was going upstairs to bed when I heard it. So I guess it would be just after eleven p.m."

Stone thanked Gault, and they went to his car, deciding the rest of the homes were too far away to be likely of any help. "At least Gault has given us something. A motorbike just after eleven. If Carlton had left the bar at ten twenty-two, he would have arrived at the school parking lot around eleven."

"I suppose you don't see that as a mere coincidence."

"Everything is connected."

She decided there was a chance the bike and the murder could be more than mere chance and didn't challenge Stone's assertion on interconnections. "Okay, let's go to where Carlton lived."

THEY DROVE TO THE OLDER HOME THAT WAS SPLIT INTO TWO levels, with the lower level rented out. A side entrance had Carlton's address on the mailbox next to the door. Knocking on the door didn't produce a response.

"Let's try the occupants at the upper portion of the house," Roberts suggested.

They walked around to the front of the house, and the doorbell did result in a heavyset man opening the door. He looked at the identification Roberts showed. "Police?" He straightened up. "What do you want?"

Roberts sensed he had visits from the police before. The middle-aged man was dressed well enough. His thinning black hair was slicked back.

"Do you know Jacob Carlton? He resides downstairs in this house."

"Yeah, we rent it out to him. Has he done something?" The tan-skinned man relaxed his posture.

"He has been murdered. What can you tell us about him?"

"Murdered? Shit, now I'll have to get another renter." His anguish passed quickly. "He lived by himself. We didn't see much of him. A couple of times we had to tell him to stop partying, but we didn't have much trouble from him. He usually paid his rent on time. Missed a day or two. Nothing much to do with him."

"Do you know his next of kin?"

The response was a shake of his head. "No, I don't think I ever saw his family."

"Do you have a key to his suite?"

"Sure. I'll get it for you. Wait here."

Roberts looked at Stone. "Do you think our landlord may not have the cleanest record?"

"Maybe. He also looks like he could have had a part in a *Godfather* movie."

They were passed a bronze-coloured key on a metal ring. "Make sure you lock up and return the key when you're done."

Stone replied, "Don't worry. I doubt this key unlocks the door to the Taj Mahal. I'll be glad to return it as soon as we're done."

———

THE ONE-BEDROOM SUITE DIDN'T COVER THE ENTIRE LOWER FLOOR. Stone suspected on the other side of one wall was the furnace and hot water tank, along with additional storage room for the upstairs owners. The suite had the smell of stale smoke, which penetrated the cushions of the mismatched furniture. The fridge contained leftover pizza and several cans of beer but was otherwise empty. The kitchen cabinets held a few boxes and cans, suitable for a quick and unhealthy meal. Stone looked at the dirty dishes in the sink and shook his head. "See anything, Anya?"

Roberts entered the kitchen from the living room, holding a plastic bag. "Just some weed. Pretty bare fixings. Not even any pictures."

"I'm sure we may find some other drugs if we look hard enough. Let's see if there's anything in the bedroom."

Roberts peered in at the bedroom from the doorway as Stone looked through the closet and the drawers. She grimaced at the unmade bed, clothes lying on a chair, and food wrappers discarded next to the bed. "Not exactly a place a woman would want to spend the night. I would say he definitely didn't have a steady girlfriend."

"Yeah, he doesn't appear to have found the key to happiness. What do you think of the landlord? Do you think he knows anything more about our victim?"

"I think he couldn't care less about what his tenant was doing unless he was making too much noise."

They returned the key to the landlord, barely answering his inquiry when he could clean out the suite and rent it again.

"That I can't tell you," Stone advised. "I suspect it depends on what the next of kin wants to do with his possessions. Until then, you're in a holding pattern."

They walked back to the car. Once inside, Roberts opened her tablet. "I have Carlton's next of kin, his parents, Joseph and Marlene Carlton. They live in Sherwood Park. Shall we go?"

"Yeah, maybe they have an idea who may have shot him. What's the address?"

"It's on Oak Street. Do you know where that is?"

"I do. I once knew a girl who lived on Oak Street."

"That I don't doubt. You seem to have known a few ladies in different places."

"I'm going to assume you meant that as a compliment."

"No comment."

Stone used the Anthony Henday ring road to arrive at one of Edmonton's bedroom communities. Sherwood Park was an oddity; even though it held a population of approximately seventy thousand people, it still held on to its status as a hamlet. The urban centre had its share of government buildings but lacked a downtown, relying on shopping centres for business and commercial activity.

Stone made his way to the address on Oak Street, a split-level home. The older home was well landscaped and looked to be well taken care of.

A tall, slim woman answered the door. Stone guessed her to be in her fifties. He showed his identification. "Marlene Carlton?"

"Yes. How can I help you?"

"May we come in?"

"Of course." She led the way to the living room. "Joe," she called out. "The police are here."

Roberts and Stone sat on the leather love seat. The furnishings were modern and well kept.

Joe, a large man, entered and sat in a matching armchair his wife was occupying. "How can we help you, Officers. Is this about Jacob?"

"I'm afraid so," Roberts answered. "He was found dead this morning, apparently from gunshot injuries."

Marlene Carlton's reaction was immediate. She covered her face with her hands and wailed. Her husband leaned back in his chair and looked up at the ceiling. Roberts and Stone waited until one of them was composed enough to speak.

Joseph Carlton spoke in a wavering voice. "Jacob always was in trouble. He seemed lost. We tried to help him but he shunned us. Now, this."

"Did he have enemies?" Roberts inquired.

"I suppose he did. We were not in touch very often."

"Does he have siblings?"

"Yes, an older brother and sister, and a younger brother. They are all successful with families. Unfortunately, they lost contact with him as well. Jacob isolated himself from them. I wish I knew why."

"Jacob looked to have a history of intoxication. Do you know if he was also involved in drugs?"

Joseph shook his head. "I don't know. We wouldn't be surprised."

"What did he do for a living?" Stone asked.

"I believe some construction work, sometimes as a roofer. He never finished school, so it was just temporary work. We offered to pay for him to go back to school, but he refused. He did allow us to pay for a lawyer when he struck and injured a pedestrian when he was drinking and driving. That was two years ago and it was one of the few times he contacted us."

"I'm sorry to hear that."

"Ironically, the lawyer was a good one and got him off on a technicality. If he had gone to prison, he might be still alive."

After leaving the Carlton's, Roberts and Stone returned to the Veloster, sitting in it as it idled.

"I feel sorry for his parents. To lose a child under any circumstances is tough." Roberts looked at her notebook. "Shall we go to the bar where the fight may have started all this?"

"Sure. A bar sounds like a good place to go to right now." He shifted the gearbox and the car lurched forward.

Stone returned to the Anthony Henday, the highway that circled Edmonton, making it easy to reach outlying areas. He had the option of going south or north to reach the west end of Edmonton. He chose the northwest route, noticing a few bikers on the highway.

"That's what I want to do this weekend. Go for a ride."

"Where to?"

"Anywhere. It doesn't matter. As long as you're on a bike, it's the journey."

"Are you going to take Cindy?" Roberts asked, referring to his present girlfriend. She knew they didn't see each other often, due to her taking university classes and working as a server at a downtown bar.

"I'll ask, but she may be busy."

"You two have made a pretty good go at it, despite your lack of together time."

"Maybe that's why it works. She doesn't have enough time with me to get bored."

Roberts smiled. "You're anything but boring. But you do have lots of other faults."

"Me? Lots of faults? No way. Name one."

She laughed, refusing to answer.

2

Paul Church strolled down the glazed stone hallway to where the small theatres were located in Grant MacEwan University campus. Originally a community college, it now offered degree courses, including those in fine arts. Church enjoyed the courses and was beginning to get involved in the university social life. The stigma of what happened in Calgary still hung over his head like a black cloud, and he hoped moving to Edmonton would give him a new start on life. Tall and good-looking, Church had maintained a quiet profile when he had first arrived in Edmonton a year ago. A few months ago, he registered for Live Theatre on a whim and to pick up a few extra course credits.

The class was small and he enjoyed the opportunity to act out different characters. Church's looks meant he didn't have a problem attracting the attention of others, although he preferred to avoid too much social activity. The acting allowed him to exercise his desire to interact with others without too much involvement. The acting classes finished a few weeks ago, but the professor, Peter McNab, informed the class they had an opportunity to use their new acting skills. He had written a play for the upcoming Edmonton Fringe Festival and he invited members of the class to be part of the play.

Church reached the small theatre, opened the door and headed down the sloping walkway to where the stage was located. He waved at the instructor, who merely glared at him for being the last to arrive. Church pulled down the spring-loaded seat and sat at the end of the line of the other seated actors.

———

Peter McNab stood in front of his troupe of actors, surveying them. His forced smile came across closer to a sneer. The sloped shoulders took away from his height and his weak posture exposed his paunch. Still, when he straightened out his back, he resembled the tall, muscular man he used to be. He was now approaching the age when his remaining soft brown hair became dominated by grey. He considered dying his hair but decided the bald spot on the top of his head would make that effort moot.

McNab adjusted his tweed jacket with leather patches on the backside of the arms. He complemented the yellow, cotton shirt underneath with khaki pants.

The actors sat bunched together in the seats normally used by the audience in the small theatre. To his back stood the stage, elevated to his waist. He breathed in the slightly stale air, attempting to speak from his stomach. McNab wanted to impress upon those in front of him that he had indeed been a Shakespearean actor at one time and that they should feel privileged that he was going to direct the play. He never understood why his writing ability was never appreciated by his peers in the acting community.

"Good afternoon everyone. I do recognize some of you from my class and as for the rest of you, I trust we will be acquainted with each other soon enough." He reached behind him and picked up a pile of stapled sets of papers resting on the stage. On the top of each set, a name had been written next to a character's name in the play. He went to each member of those sitting in front of him and gave each a particular copy of the play.

To his far left he handed the first stapled document to Mitch Donnelly, who slouched with one ankle resting on his knee. His worn clothing seemed at odds with the pretty woman next to him. He considered Donnelly a moody, brooding type. McNab had chosen him to play the role of a nervous, weak man. He suspected Donnelly would be upset at not being the leading man. He had hinted during their classroom skits he thought of himself in that light. *But I need a man with more physical stature. Mitch may have a strong personality but my play needs a leading man that looks like one.*

As he passed the next set of papers to Tanya Conner it didn't escape McNab's attention that Donnelly cursed at reading who he was to play. Conner, as much as he could tell, was Donnelly's girlfriend. At least they always sat next to each other, although McNab didn't see much interaction between them. None of the whispered comments or hand holding one would expect from a couple.

Conner brushed back some loose hair that had crept over one of her eyes as she took the offered manuscript. Unlike Donnelly she thanked him and seemed excited as she looked at her role. Her posture followed the cushioned chair and she kept her tight blue-jeaned legs folded perfectly at the knees. Her loose top was a light enough material to show off her curves.

Next to Conner sat Dana Sharpe. McNab was conflicted in the role he assigned her. Sometimes she exhibited great energy and enthusiasm and other times disappeared as if she was a field mouse. Now she didn't slouch in the chair as much as scrunch into it. She wore jean shorts, sandals, and an open shirt over a tank top. Although not tall, she did possess a good figure. He finally decided on a small role but also one that required her to be an aggressive character. McNab hoped she could step into that role without dropping back into her quiet mood unexpectedly. She took the papers from him without comment, barely looking up as she reached out her hand. She did quickly scan the page where her name was printed to her character's name.

There was an empty seat next to Sharpe, but one seat over was a woman in her thirties. She was checking her mobile when McNab approached her. Unlike the other women, she wore a skirt and kept her legs crossed at the ankles. Brenda Thompson kept her shoulder-length dirty-blonde hair neat. She wasn't a student in his class but she had explained to him she was currently employed at a pharmacy and liked to take courses, wanting to learn about something, *anything*, other than counting pills. When she read that the well-known professor of Live Theatre was accepting applications for his murder play, she decided to seek him out in his office and apply in person. McNab noted she lacked acting experience, but her friendly face coupled with her saying he was well-known, won him over. Thompson added she wanted excitement in her life and believed the play would help her accomplish that goal.

Sitting next to Thompson was another non-student of his. The older, heavyset man was an electrician by trade and helped build sets for amateur plays. McNab recalled the nervous man requesting a part in his play, expressing that just a small part would do. McNab didn't think much of Tyler Burgess, wondering why a man without any acting experience would think he should ask for a part. However, as it turned out, there was a part for an older man in his play and Burgess would fit the physical description quite well. McNab passed the papers to a shaking hand.

McNab paused a moment as he stepped in front of the next actor. Jessica Knowles was pretty and she knew it. McNab tried to look casual as he handed over the play to her. His eyes quickly glanced down at her sleeveless top, showing off her slender arms. She gave McNab a friendly smile of perfect teeth and red lips as she accepted the offered document.

The final recipient of his play was Paul Church. McNab didn't know too much about the quiet, well-mannered man. His class, Live Theatre, was small enough to note there was tension between Church and the lovely Knowles. He assumed Church had been either rude or had become too aggressive to his favourite student. He put his dislike to Church aside and gave him the main male lead. Despite his lack of acting experience, Church did look like a leading man, possessing both height and a handsome face.

McNab returned to the front of the stage.

"You now all have copies of the play and I would appreciate it if it is not shown to anyone not in the play. I worked hard on writing *Death of a Philanderer* and I don't want someone else borrowing ideas for their own use." He stared at his audience, wanting to ensure they understood he was sincere. Tyler Burgess pinched his eyebrows as he stared back at him. McNab recognized Burgess as the man who stammered out his request to have a part in his play and briefly considered asking him if he had a comment to make. He wanted everyone to understand that he, Peter McNab, was the writer and director of the play, and would be maintaining complete control of its production. He decided against giving Burgess a chance to speak during his address.

"I have taken the initiative of assigning roles to each of you, as I'm sure you have noted in your handout. If you *strongly* feel that you are better suited for a different role, we can discuss the matter in private later." He paused, letting the words sink into the troupe. "Good. I would like to run through our first rehearsal tomorrow morning, *promptly* at ten in this theatre. Do study your lines. We will do a walk-through of the actions, but the main thing is to be the character outlined in your script *and* to remember your lines. I have one bit of good news to bestow upon you. The Fringe has decided my play was worthy enough to be given a proper venue and not merely a space created out in one of the drinking establishments. Our performance will be at the Walterdale Theatre." He beamed and had hoped for applause but settled for the pleased looks on the actors' faces.

The group left, chatting among themselves, save for one woman. Knowles stood, waiting for the others to leave before she approached him. She shook her short hair away from her face as she smiled up at him. She saw his eyes quickly dart to the V-neck of her thin T-shirt and to her powder-blue jean shorts. She expected that reaction from him and other men and was amused how they often offered small courtesies to her.

"Ms. Knowles, what can I do for you?"

She paused before speaking, waiting for his eyes to fix on her own. "You have me as the stage director and general stagehand."

"Is that a problem? I assigned you to that position because I believed you to be the best qualified for handling the stage. I know you have acting experience but I thought I'd give you an opportunity to try the director's role. You would be working with me much of the time and I could give you advice now and then."

"I appreciate that." She gave a self-indulgent smile. "What I wanted to ask is if you can make sure I have access to the storage facilities here and later at the Walterdale Theatre."

"Yes, of course."

"Good, that's all I wanted to ask." She gave him a smile and waved her fingers goodbye, strolling past the chairs to the exit.

McNab watched the doors close behind her, slowly releasing his breath.

————

CONNER WALKED BETWEEN CHURCH AND DONNELLY DOWN THE hallway. "I'm really excited about the part I have. This is going to be so much fun. I guess Paul and I will have a scene together." She looked up at him, deciding he really did look like a leading man. Conner began to imagine what it would be like to enact some of the scenes with him on stage.

Donnelly interjected. "I wonder how McNab picks which part we get? Tossing names in a hat? I sure got a crap role."

Conner reached for his hand, which he quickly shook off. "Oh, Mitch, I'm sure he studied our resumes and made a decision according to experience and how he saw a character would best fit us. You're just starting out as an actor and he doesn't know your abilities yet."

Church added, "I have a feeling McNab has not written or produced a lot of plays. Maybe he picked the parts because he doesn't have a lot of practical experience in the theatre."

Conner touched Church's arm with her fingers. "I think you're right." She paused, licking her lips. "You know, perhaps we could practice our lines before the first rehearsal. I doubt McNab is going to be patient with any errors. The three of us could do a quick run-through."

Church agreed. "Sounds okay with me. When and where?"

Conner turned to Donnelly. "You'll join us, won't you? It'll be good for you to practice with us."

"Nah, I don't want to waste time on that. I can learn my lines easy enough later. Besides, it's wing and beer night at First Round Bar."

————

CONNER AND CHURCH FOUND AN EMPTY CLASSROOM, DECIDING IT was a good place to rehearse.

She followed the script's action line and did a spin around on the laminate floor. "Okay, I'm now conversing with Nicolas just as you return with drinks."

Church walked across the floor as Conner spoke to an imaginary person.

"Oh, well, perhaps some time we could. I'm really busy lately, so I'm not sure when we can get together."

Church stood close by, pretending to hold glasses in his hand.

Conner laughed. "Where's my wine? Did you drink it carrying it over here?"

"The bottle was empty. What else would you like to have?" Church acted like he was handing a drink to someone next to Conner.

"I believe there's more wine in the kitchen. I'll take a look." Conner turned and walked to the front of the classroom where the desk for an instructor was located.

"All right, the script says I watch you walk to the kitchen." He chuckled. "I guess that means either my character likes yours or she has a very interesting walk."

Conner laughed. "So maybe I need to try to make my walk a little more exaggerated." She returned to where Church stood and walked again to the front of the classroom, this time swaying her hips more.

"Now that was eye-catching. Since this is supposed to be a semi-comedy, maybe you should use that walk during the play."

"That's a possibility. Depends on what McNab has to say about it. I guess my character is supposed to be a bit sleazy."

"I like it." He looked back at the script and read out loud, "I should go and help her." Church stepped to where Conner stood.

Conner pretended to hold up a bottle of wine. "See, I know where the wine is kept." She positioned herself by the desk.

"A smart girl like you likely knows a lot of things." Church hesitated. "Here, I'm to put my arm around your waist and lean into you."

"Okay, let's act this out." She waited as he positioned his hand behind her back and bent her back slightly. She glanced at the paper she held in one hand just over his shoulder. "Now I have to ask, are you going to start something you can't finish? Because it seems to me that you just might be the teasing type."

"The rest of this script has us kissing and then, I rip open your blouse." Church felt warm breath from her slightly parted lips.

"We're going to have to kiss on stage eventually." Conner used a hand behind his neck to pull his head down. After one short kiss, he returned for a longer kiss.

Church continued to hold her close.

Conner gasped out another part of the play. "Okay, let's say you've already ripped open my shirt. Then I say, Oh! You're such a bad boy." Conner stared at him, lowering the paper in her hand.

"But you like it." He looked at the desk. "I guess we can use this as the kitchen table." Church put his hands on her waist and easily lifted her on the desk. He was mildly surprised as she lay on her back and spread her legs, following the direction of the script. Church climbed on the desk on his knees between her legs and looked down at her. "Okay, here the lights go off and the scene ends."

"Well, that sure is going to be an interesting scene. It could be almost X-rated if they don't turn off the set lights quick enough. I've never been ravished on the stage before." She laughed as she looked at him, aware he hadn't made any motion to remove himself from the desk, restricting her ability to get off the desk.

"I'm lucky. I get to kiss the prettiest girl in the play."

Conner giggled. "Thanks. I think we're going to work well together." She lifted herself to her elbows. She saw Church take the hint and move off the desk, offering his hand to help her down.

He scanned the script. "So, it looks like we have an incident in the kitchen, causing the table to tumble on its side. Others rush into the kitchen, and later we move into the living room. Then, soon after I get killed."

"And you reappear as the detective. You get two roles."

"True." He scanned the script. "Hmm, I do get to check you for a weapon."

"Careful there, I'm ticklish."

"I'll remember that." He hesitated and tried to sound casual as he asked, "Hey, do you want to go for a drink?"

"Sure, I have some free time."

They walked out of the classroom and down the hallway.

"So, are you seeing anyone, Paul?"

"No, no one. I take it you're going out with Mitch."

"Well, I guess so. I'm not sure about him at times. Like he seems indifferent to what I'm doing and my likes. I don't expect him to take an interest in everything I do, but Mitch is a bit too focused on his own needs."

They walked outside, crossing 104th Avenue at 107th Street. Church looked up. The sky had patches of blue interspersed among tall white clouds with dark centres. "Shit, it looks like the forecast was right. It was clear this morning."

"A little rain won't hurt anyone. In fact, sometimes it's fun to walk in the rain."

Church chuckled. "Can I assume then that you have entered wet T-shirt contests in the past?"

She punched him on the shoulder. "What kind of girl do you think I am? And don't answer that." She laughed. "You have a dirty mind."

They turned along the avenue to The Great Canadian Brewhouse. The inside of the bar was half-full and noisy. TVs showed various sports programs without sound. They sat at a high-top table and were soon approached by a friendly server, who quickly took their order.

"So, have you done much acting?" Church asked.

"I've done a few school plays in high school and then a few more now and then. Like a small part in a dinner theatre. I did a Fringe play last year and decided I wanted to have that experience again. I know our esteemed instructor is full of himself but I thought the outline of his play sounded intriguing. I was glad he gave me a main role. How about you? What's your acting background?"

He laughed. "None. I don't know why I took the acting course or why I applied to be in the play."

"So, let me get this straight. No acting experience, no burning desire to be in McNab's play, and yet you get the leading man role?"

"Yeah, I guess that was rather fortunate to get that part."

"If Mitch knew that, he would be even more upset. He wanted to be the leading man." She shook her head. "He doesn't understand that acting experience, which you have none and he has some, isn't the only criteria. For this play, the leading man needs to have a more commanding presence. You're tall, among other attributes, and Mitch isn't." She tossed her hair back as she looked at his reaction.

"Oh." He took a drink of his beer. "Well, I guess I didn't understand the reason before why I was given the role."

"I'm glad we're going to be working together. It'll be fun."

She thought about Mitch briefly. Most men gave Tanya a second glance but Donnelly hardly acknowledged her. She did like men who didn't fawn all over her and treat her like a princess. On the other hand, she was getting a bit tired of him taking her for granted. He did have a jealous streak and was easily offended if he felt he wasn't being respected. *If Mitch knew what I was thinking about Paul, he would want to kill us both.*

3

THE PARKING LOT OF THE DRAGONHEAD'S BAR AND GRILL consisted of uneven asphalt, with faded yellow parking lines that didn't appear to serve any purpose. Bits of broken glass littered the lot, along with a couple of crushed beer cans. The bar was located along a strip mall, featuring a walk-in medical clinic, a tanning studio, a daycare, and a convenience store. The mixed grouping of stores meant the parking lot was nearly always full. Stone found a spot facing the street and scanned the lot.

"Looks like a lovely place to have a party," he commented sarcastically.

"I guess it depends on your definition of a party. Perhaps there are different types of festivities done here. Such as using drugs."

They entered the dimly lit bar. A server was in the process of restoring chairs back on the floor from where they rested on a table top. Stone approached her on the slightly damp floor.

"Good morning. Is the manager here?"

The long-haired brunette gave him a curious look, and after apparently deciding he was worthy of being given the required information, pointed toward where the bar and kitchen resided at the back. "His name is Curtis. Just call out to the kitchen. He's making up a food order."

Stone and Roberts reached the bar. Beyond the clean stone surface were various bottles. To the right was the kitchen area. After Stone called his name, a tall blond man appeared.

"Yes?" Curtis carried a clipboard with an order form attached and a pen.

Stone showed his identification, introducing Roberts and himself. "We understand there was an altercation last Friday night where the police had to be called."

Curtis shrugged. "Yes. Nothing too unusual there. A scuffle broke out in the bar, so we kicked them outside. We called the police as a matter of course."

"Were they regulars?"

"Not really. I think I've seen them here before."

"Did the two groups know each other?" Roberts asked.

Curtis shook his head. "Not likely. They arrived at different times. The server for their section said only one guy was drinking heavily and was tossing back shooters. The rest only had one or two drinks. The guy drinking heavily was the one causing problems, shooting off his mouth."

"But you kicked all of them out?"

"Bar policy. We don't differentiate on who starts fights, just get them out where they can do less harm to the other patrons."

"Anything you can tell us? Like how the fight started."

"The server overheard them. I guess one group was making comments about the woman sitting at the other table."

"Okay, do you have any videos?" Stone asked.

"We have videos from inside the bar and from the front entrance. I can get you copies."

"Please."

Curtis started to walk to his office and paused. "What happened afterward? We don't usually get a police investigation after a fight."

Roberts informed him, "One those in the bar fight was shot later that night. So this is now a murder investigation."

Curtis cursed and went to his office located on the other side of the bar near the entrance. He returned a few minutes later with two DVD discs. "Sorry, I don't have any flash drives. I trust the police still can play discs."

"We have equipment to play not only discs, but also tape, both VHS and Beta." Stone then added, "You would not believe how old some of the CCTV equipment is that's still used. Thanks for your help."

Roberts commented as they left the bar, "At least the manager was cooperative. I've never understood why people, other than someone guilty of the crime, are so reluctant to help the police with an investigation."

Stone retorted, "Maybe because everyone is guilty of something. Trust issues I suppose."

"I guess you're right. Let's take a look at the videos and see if anything stands out."

———

THEY RETURNED TO THE DOWNTOWN OFFICE AND STONE SETTLED back in a squeaky five-legged office chair. "Okay, let's see what happened inside the bar first."

One of the grainy videos showed reasonable detail, considering the lights in the bar were kept low. The images showed the bar had an assortment of tables. In the centre of the bar, round high-top tables held four barstools each, while the rest of the bar held low-level square tables. Some of the lower tables were joined together to form rectangular tables. A second video showed the far back of the bar; two pool tables sat on a raised floor. Two men were playing, drinking from beer bottles between turns.

Stone's and Roberts's attention went back to the first video where two of the low-top tables were situated close to each other. Four men sat around one table, with three of them wearing baseball caps. One of the ball-cap-wearing men stood out from the rest, looking older and scruffier than the others. He had a lighter complexion than his companions and was taking liquor shots as well as beer.

The table next to them consisted of two older, heavyset men, and a slimmer, well-endowed woman. Her long dark hair had blonde streaks. Her face looked like she was approaching thirty, but she was dressed as if she was younger. Time passed, and the woman stood and walked toward the back of the bar.

Stone and Roberts watched, not seeing anything unusual. The other tables were partially filled, although the bar was gradually filling up as the evening progressed. In the background, two couples sat around a high-top table, slowly consuming drinks. The waitress moved efficiently from table to table, dropping off drinks while picking up empty glasses. She stopped to chat briefly with a single woman wearing a black coat, sitting at one of the tall tables. Behind her, two men wearing long-sleeved work shirts shared a pitcher of beer.

The streaked-haired woman returned, walking slowly past the tables. She turned her head as she passed the group of four men, apparently reacting to a comment. One of the two men she sat with said something in return, and words were quickly exchanged between the two groups. The argument quickly escalated, with both groups standing up, pointing fingers. The bar manager and another larger man, who wore a T-shirt with *Security* written on it, quickly rushed over and began to push the combatants toward the exit doors.

Roberts switched over to the video feed from outside. The security T-shirt man stepped between the groups, taking turns pushing one individual at a time away from the others. One of the heavier-set men pulled a knife, causing the security man to hold up his hands to him, shouting something at the knife holder. For a minute the two groups jawed at each other with the security man bravely standing between them. In the background, a few bar patrons were walking quickly away, heading to where vehicles were parked.

Flashing police lights appeared at the edge of the video. Two police cars came to a stop and police officers began the process of taking things under control.

"Okay, that appears to be it," Roberts commented. "According to the report, all names were taken down and a knife was confiscated."

"So the fight starts when one table makes comments about a woman sitting at the other table. Six guys and they start to fight over a woman."

"Women, they do cause disturbances."

"Don't you dare start blaming women for men acting like idiots."

"So, you're saying there's no correlation between women and bar fights?" He raised his eyebrows.

"I'm saying in the bar men can act like imbeciles without the help of women."

"Ah, you're likely right there." He chuckled.

"Let's stop for a bite to eat. I have a feeling this is going to be a long day."

"Sure. Tim Horton's is close by."

Roberts looked at her phone and answered it.

Stone walked with her to his car, opening the door for her as she continued to chat. He started the motor and was already on the road when she hung up.

"Well?"

"That was the cop who did the report. He said it was more yapping than fighting and they did confiscate a knife but it wasn't used in the fight. The owner was just waving it around. Only one person seemed under the influence of alcohol and he was the loudest of the group. That was our victim, Jacob Carlton. They told him he had too much to drink and wasn't allowed to drive. They offered to drive him home, but he refused, swearing at them as well.

"The rest of the two groups were okay, not drunk, and were happy to drop the fighting. So, it seems the loudmouth was the one who ended up being killed. Maybe someone in the other group wasn't that happy to drop the matter."

"Could be. Maybe Carlton had pissed off others besides the ones in the bar." Stone drummed his fingers on the steering wheel.

"Well, the cop checked his record. He had a history of unsocial behaviour. He has had three driving-under-the-influence convictions, including one where he left the victim permanently disabled. He probably has made a few enemies along the way."

"Maybe the bar fight was due to something that happened in the past. Someone in the other group recognized him and decided it was time for revenge."

"It sounds plausible. Shall we do the interviews?"

"Yeah, after some coffee and food."

They finished their coffee and sandwich at the coffee shop. The place was noisy but efficient with taking their order and having it ready. They sat at one of the practical tables with sturdy chairs. A man sat at a neighbouring table, working on a newspaper's crossword puzzles.

Stone commented. "Crosswords are like investigating murders."

"How so?" Roberts gave him a questioning look.

"The clues are all obscure and sometimes don't seem to be related to each other."

They returned to the car with Stone carrying his extra-large coffee with him.

"It appears that those involved in the bar fight didn't live far from the Dragonhead's Bar and Grill." Roberts looked at the list of names and addresses.

"Which is the closest?" Stone asked as he started the car.

"Thane Hunter." She read off the address

Stone drove to the address, one of the townhouses in a long row of clones. The small patch of lawn between the cracked sidewalks looked desperate for water. Children ran around in circles on a neighbouring lot, having forgotten who was chasing who. A dog looked up a concrete step as the detectives stepped out of the vehicle and dropped his head again. The older lab had learned to stay away from children that liked to pull his tail and ignore people moving with purpose. Neither was likely to feed him and more than likely just annoy him.

They rang the doorbell, and a woman carrying an infant allowed them to enter after they identified themselves. The blonde-haired woman looked tired and had stopped caring what she wore. A toddler stood by a chair, rolling a small plastic car back and forth across the seat cushion. He looked up briefly and continued with the tire endurance test.

In a love seat, a big man waited, a beer can in hand. Unkempt brown hair sprayed out from his Patriots baseball cap. He completed his fashion statement with a beer T-shirt and dark jeans.

"Thane Hunter?" Roberts asked.

He nodded and swept a hand to the couch.

Roberts inspected the couch first before sitting down. "Can you go over the altercation last night with us?"

"Just as I told the cops last night. The assholes started to hassle us. We told them to piss off, and then they wanted to take it to another level.

The bar kicked us out, and there we were jawing and shoving. At the time, I didn't think too much of it. Stan and I can handle ourselves. We just wanted to make sure Stan's girlfriend, Izzy, didn't get involved."

"All right, but you pulled a knife for starters. I understand there was some general yelling and threats. Your two groups break apart and supposedly go your separate ways. All is good then, but an hour later, someone is dead from a gunshot."

"Someone's dead? Shit, we didn't have anything to do with that." Hunter shifted his bulk on the couch.

"Maybe so, but understandably, we have an interest in details. What did you see and hear? A man is dead, so we're looking at murder charges. I understand the police took a knife from you. Care to comment?"

"Yeah, but I didn't use it last night."

"Didn't you wave it around?"

"Yeah, just as a warning for them to back off, or there would be serious trouble. I never swung it at them, let alone cut anyone."

"Does that mean forensics won't find traces of blood on it?"

"It's a knife, ain't it? There may be blood, but not from any fight last night. Besides, the guy was shot, wasn't he? What the hell does a knife have to do with it?"

"Simple. A fight broke out. Guns and knives are weapons. If you're willing to use a knife, then maybe a gun is your next step."

"I didn't use no gun. Neither did Stan. You can take that to the bank."

"Do you own a gun?"

"No." He elaborated, "I did, but sold it a couple years ago. It was a shotgun for hunting."

Roberts asked, sounding exasperated, "Okay, what did you see that night in and out of the bar? Anyone taking interest in your altercation?"

Hunter shook his head. "None that I noticed. Look, me, Stan, and Izzy just went to the bar for a couple of beers and maybe play some pool. Before we even finished our first round, we get harassed and end up outside. A few minutes later, the cops come by and start asking questions. That's it. I know nothing more."

They left the townhouse and Stone asked, "What do you think of Hunter?"

"Not the most useful interview I've had. He said he didn't do it, and if that's true, maybe that makes his buddy, Stan, the number one suspect."

"Possibly, but he did defend Stan. Thing is, he never even got out of that chair when we came in. Pretty relaxed, no sign of stress. He comes across as too lazy to commit murder like there's so much effort in even pulling a knife."

Their next visit was at a walk-up apartment. The brick exterior didn't promise anything special on the inside and it delivered. The end stairwell was too warm from the incoming sun, and the carpet released flavours from a thousand people. Roberts rapped on the door, and Stan Knox opened the door immediately.

The sandy-haired man was almost Hunter's height but considerably lighter. The inside of the apartment surprised Stone. It was clean with decent-looking furniture. Izzy, a dark-haired woman, offered them coffee that they declined.

Moss guessed that Izzy had migrated to Canada when he heard her speak. Her slim figure was offset by her top and he immediately considered implants.

Moss assumed Hunter had phoned Knox to inform him the police were investigating a murder but he still informed him of their investigation. "According to the police, you were involved in a bar altercation last night. Lots of talk, some pushing, and a knife was drawn. Sometime later, one of the men you were arguing with was found dead. Care to comment on that?"

Knox wasn't as relaxed as Hunter but gave his version of the events in a rambling dialogue. "... and after a bit of shoving, we started to move apart. That was it. When we got outside, they lost their courage."

"Are you saying it wasn't Thane or yourself that used a gun?"

"That's what I'm saying. If one of them got shot later, it wasn't by us. One of them was blitzed or on drugs. Hyper in the bar."

"How did the fight start in the bar?"

"The assholes were yapping about Izzy's tits. I told them to shut the fuck up."

"So that led to what happened outside. Anyone else have a weapon?"

"Thane pulled his but kept it low. Not in a fighting position. I don't carry a knife."

"Okay, so you're all acting like it's a bad West Side Story movie. What happens next?"

"The bar must have called the cops. We see blue lights, and suddenly, cop cars are blazing down on us. The cops take down our names and tell us to go home, so we did."

"Do you own a gun?"

"Yeah, but not here. I have a rifle on my dad's farm."

Stone asked, "Izzy, what did you see? Can you add anything to the events?"

She shook her head. "No, when we went outside, I stood behind Stan. I didn't want those other men to see me."

"Okay, thanks for your information. We may be in contact later."

They left the apartment and Roberts asked, "Well, what do think now?"

"I'm willing to bet that Stan and company are telling the truth. Which makes me want to talk to the others."

"Think they know more about who shot their friend?"

"Good possibility. It may be amateur hour with guns, knives, and fools." He started his car, and after a short drive, stopped at a convenience store. "I'm still hungry. Want anything?"

"No, I'm good." She waited in the car, and shortly later, he came out munching on a hot dog. She watched him gulp down the hot dog and follow it with a bottle of water. "Do you know what they put in hot dogs?"

"I'm pretending I don't know, and please, don't tell me."

"As long as you enjoyed it."

"Mustard covers up a lot of sins."

Their next stop was an older two-story home in need of renovations but not ill cared for.

The doorbell was answered by a middle-aged woman, who stood behind the screen door. She looked at them without saying a word and appeared ready to win any staring contest.

Stone produced his police identification. "I'm Detective Moss Stone and this my partner, Anya Roberts. We're looking for Samuel and Diego Martinez. Are they in?"

The woman gasped and took a half step back. With a shaking hand, she pushed open the screen door and began shouting into the house.

The nervous woman escorted the detectives into the living room. She pointed for them to sit on a pair of chairs that suited the rest of the older-style furniture. The interview with two brothers, one just a year older than the other, was closely monitored by their parents, a grandfather, two sisters, and a younger brother.

Stone was happy to let Roberts conduct the questioning. He breathed in the spicy air, deciding it might have been a mistake to eat the hot dog.

Each question Roberts asked was translated and repeated to the grandfather, and the two suspects conferred between themselves in whispered comments before the older one replied.

"Tell me what happened at the Dragonhead's Bar last night."

Samuel had the same nervous-looking face as his mother. "We were sitting at a table, and something happened, and we got into an argument with the next table. The bar manager didn't like us arguing and kicked everyone out. The police came."

Roberts considered the missing details of the *Reader's Digest* version. "But the reason the argument started was because *your* table was making rude comments about a woman sitting at the other table. Isn't that true?"

Samuel nodded and received an angry finger waving from the mother.

"The police said a knife was pulled outside the bar."

"Samuel!" The father spoke, his eyes wide with anger.

"It wasn't us! I swear."

Roberts wasn't sure if the denial was to her or to the enraged parent. "Yes, the police confirm that. However, that tells us it may have not been a simple argument. In fact, your friend Jacob Carlton was found dead this morning."

Samuel's mouth dropped open. "I don't know this."

"He was gunned down a few blocks from his home." Roberts studied Samuel's and Diego's faces, looking for a sign one already knew of his death.

"We don't know anything about a shooting."

"But you left the bar together. Didn't one of you contact him later when you arrived home? A phone call or text to see if he was all right? Are you sure you want to stick to that story? Because if it turns out we did find out you did see or know something later, you will be charged with obstruction. Understand? That means prison."

That resulted in a thousand words between parents, the suspects, and the grandfather. Finally, the older boy spoke again.

"I was standing next to Jacob. Then, suddenly we saw the lights of the police. They took our names and told us not to cause any more trouble. We then went home. I didn't know Jacob was shot."

"And you didn't try to check with him later that night?"

The older brother shook his head.

"Why not? He was your friend. You almost got into a fight in the bar, had to give your name to the police, and didn't even check with him? Are you sure you were his friend?"

More conversation among the family members ensued. Finally, the father spoke.

"I apologize. We do not mean to make your investigation difficult. Our sons have not been honest with us where they went last night and what they did." He stopped to stare at them momentarily and then clasped his hands in front of him as he returned his attention to Roberts. "This boy who died, we did not like him being with our sons. He was older, and he just liked to party. No responsibility. We have only one cell phone in our family. For emergencies. I would not like my sons calling him. This, at least, they do what I wish."

"Do you know anyone who would cause Jacob harm? Any history with him?"

The father shook his head. "No, he not come to the house but once. He could tell I didn't like him, so he would meet up with my boys later. Now at least my sons know that when I say someone is up to no good, I am right." He pointed at his chest for emphasis.

Roberts thanked them for their time, leaving her business card if they remembered any more information.

"Man, it's good to get out of that house. I could barely breath in there."

"I didn't mind it. I think you're just a little sensitive to food right now, thanks to the hot dog."

"Okay, you're awarded one official I-told-you-so. We're running out of people to talk to about that shooting. Those two boys looked too scared of their parents to do anything with a gun."

"Maybe the killing wasn't related to the bar altercation."

"True, which will make it that much harder to solve."

"Okay, next stop is Samuel and Diego's friend. I'm not optimistic about getting much information from him."

———

KELLY NOSTRUM WAS EDGY WHEN THE DETECTIVES ARRIVED AT HIS apartment. He lived on the main floor, which featured a view of the parking lot from the dark living room. He shared the apartment with an equally anxious girlfriend.

Stone assessed Nostrum as a human jackrabbit, ready to jump at the first sign of trouble. He watched his left-hand shake as he took a drink from a can of pop. Stone decided to direct his questioning as if Nostrum did know something.

"We know you and your buddies got into a confrontation at the Dragonhead's Bar last night. So much so, the bar kicked you out, and the police were called. And guess what? One of the guys *you* were fighting with was murdered last night. We know Jacob Carlton died from a gunshot wound. The murder weapon has not been found yet, but that's not unexpected." He relaxed on the couch next to Roberts, peering at Nostrum as his girlfriend stood and twitched next to him.

"We have eliminated a lot of the suspects that night, and now, we are here. You, my friend, have a couple of options. One, you could pretend you didn't do anything wrong that night, that you don't know how Jacob died. In that case, you better pray that gun stays hidden. I'm sure there are fingerprints on it." He saw the girlfriend gasp and Nostrum retreat farther into the chair, shaking his head. "Your other option is to tell us what happened, right now. The difference could be between murder and involuntary manslaughter." He counted two heartbeats. "Well?"

Nostrum's voice broke. "We heard the cops coming. I turned to see them. I didn't do anything. I know nothing about the shooting. I don't even like going to that bar. From now on, I'm going to stay at home." His girlfriend hugged his neck, causing Stone to worry about Nostrum's safety.

"Have you ever seen the other group before?"

"No. I just went to the bar to play some pool. I've never been in a fight in a bar before."

Roberts and Stone left after leaving a card in the vague hope Nostrum remembered anything.

Stone mumbled as they headed to the car. "All those interviews did was to create more paperwork." He sighed and mumbled, "Any chance we could claim this was a suicide?"

She laughed. "Not likely. Maybe when the examiner's office is finished, we'll have more information to work on. Are you planning to work on the case tomorrow or are you going to relax on the weekend?"

"I think I'll go for a ride on Saturday. Weather is supposed to be good, so I'll take advantage of it. How about you?"

"I'm supposed to get together with some girlfriends. It should be fun. I haven't been able to see some of them for a while. Be careful on that bike. And don't speed."

He raised his eyebrows. "Me, speed?"

"I've been in your car. You push the limits."

"I'll be in full control of my bike on a nice divided highway. What possibly could go wrong?"

"The laws of chance finally catching up to you, that's what."

"Point taken."

4

A QUICK TWIST OF THE WRIST REVVED UP THE BIKE'S MOTOR AS IT
sat at the stop line. Moss Stone hated the traffic lights that ran along the
main road through Spruce Grove, another small city close to Edmonton.
On weekdays, the highway was filled with traffic for the twenty-minute
drive between the cities as commuters jogged to arrive at their destination
as quickly as possible. The weekend had a much lower level of traffic.
Stone, after coming off Highway 16A where he pushed past the hundred-
kilometres-an-hour speed limit, dropped the big bike's speed down to
eighty, then sixty. He rolled through the first set of traffic lights and came
to a stop at Century Road.

It seemed to him he always had to stop at the Century Road traffic
lights. He knew the laws of probability stated that at least occasionally the
lights should be green as he approached the intersection but the universe
had other ideas.

Long seconds ticked by. Before the green light gave him the okay to
move forward, the left-turn advance arrows flashed. Four vehicles turned,
clearing the left-turn lane. The arrow continued to flash, set on a timer
that benefited no one.

The lights turned green and his bike quickly moved up to the sixty-
kilometres-an-hour speed limit. The speed limit was set arbitrarily low for

reasons unknown, annoying most drivers. Photo radar, at each intersection, helped to ensure compliance. It didn't really matter to Stone what the speed limit was. He knew from experience he would have to stop at the next set of lights. The same devious people who set the speed limit also made sure the traffic lights were synchronized to turn red for vehicles as they approached each intersection. In a feat that required precision timing, the traffic lights were synchronized to turn red at each set of traffic lights in both the westbound and eastbound directions.

Stone switched to the inside lane, believing it would be a bit faster. He checked the side mirrors of his bike and spotted two other bikes. The closer bike, a big highway bike similar to his own, was about a block behind in the right-hand lane. The two riders, each wearing black helmets and black leather outerwear, slowly advanced with the traffic. The other bike was farther behind and appeared much smaller in the convex mirror. He couldn't discern any details but was under the impression the red bike was designed for quickness and not long trips. It sported a lone rider who wore a dark blue helmet.

Several cars and trucks waited at the Calahoo Road intersection, another set of traffic lights. Time slowed as a few vehicles moved along the main road. Another set of left-turn advanced lights flashed. A pause after they ceased before the traffic lights turned green. He followed the slow parade of cars in front of him. For a brief moment, he reached sixty-five kilometres an hour before the brake lights of the car in front of them indicated they had reached the next set of traffic lights.

Jennifer Heil Way was the last set of lights before the open road. It didn't mean he could reach highway speed yet. He checked his mirrors again, seeing both bikes. The red bike had closed the gap. After another long wait, the green light allowed the traffic to proceed. The road became a highway in appearance but not in the speed limit. Eighty kilometres an hour was deemed fast enough. An RCMP car waited between the east and west lanes. The highly trained officer pointed the radar gun at the traffic, ready to punish anyone with a ticket who believed they were a safe driver above the appointed limit.

Stone knew the RCMP officers had little sympathy for traffic violations for those on bikes. The fact he was a city detective was best not ventured forth as a method of defence. In the hierarchy of police departments, the RCMP believed they were at the top and, occasionally, felt the need to exert that position.

A pickup truck was behind him, closing the space between them rapidly. He moved to the right lane, letting the less patient driver take the risk of a speeding ticket. In his mirror, he saw the other two bikes, with the red bike now passing the bigger road bike.

A few kilometres later, the turnoff for the town of Stony Plain appeared, and shortly after that, the highway finally allowed the speeds for which it was designed. Stone kept his speed almost twenty kilometres per hour above the speed limit. In his experience, he wasn't likely to get a ticket; police usually had a tolerance on the highway for faster-moving traffic within reason. The highway bike had dropped farther behind, not appearing to be in any hurry. The red bike rapidly accelerated but, before overtaking him, turned off on the ramp to Stony Plain.

Cruising down the highway, Stone felt the rumble of the 1200 cc engine. He still exercised caution about his speed, not wanting to get a ticket on the warm, sunny day. The weather forecast promised a great weekend and he knew he had taken advantage of it by riding his bike. The Harley Davidson was a few years old, but because he was limited on how often he used it, it still had low kilometres on it. He glanced at his side mirror, looking for any vehicles that may be part of the traffic control. Trucks and various nondescript cars made up the rear view, along with the other road bike.

Highway 16A merged into Highway 16, becoming the Yellowhead Highway. Traffic became denser, as the heavier trucks joined the four lanes of traffic. Stone accelerated his bike to the right lane, knowing his turnoff was soon approaching. Highway 43, also known as the Alaskan Highway, went to the northwest corner of the province. He certainly wasn't planning to travel that far but he did increase his speed after turning north. He passed a few cars, several pickup trucks and a couple of truck-trailer units. He checked his side mirror again, not seeing anything unusual, other than the motorbike with the two riders. They maintained the gap between Stone and themselves.

A few kilometres later, he reached Highway 633, turning left onto the secondary highway. There, he quickly jumped up to cruising speed and beyond.

The speed was a bit of a risk on the two-lane road as there could be vehicles using his lane to pass in the opposite direction, but one he had calculated he could take. Too soon he reached Range Road 33, turning right to enter the village of Alberta Beach, located on the shore of Lac Sainte Anne.

The village, with a population of less than a thousand permanent residents, was a destination on weekends for those who wanted to get away from the city. Despite its small size, Alberta Beach had three restaurants, all serving good food. One, in particular, was his destination, known for its burgers.

Jungle's Bar and Grill was usually busy during the summer and this day was no exception. He stopped his bike, took off his helmet, and relaxed for a moment. There were a few trucks, cars, and bikes parked in the small parking lot. As he walked up to the restaurant, he recognized a few people sitting outside and waved to them. They had arrived on bikes as well and he knew them only through Alberta Beach. They didn't know he was a detective and he preferred to keep that information to himself.

He ordered a cheeseburger and beer and carried them to the outside table where the others sat.

"Hey, Stone, we wondered what happened to you. You've been hiding out somewhere?" Big Tom grinned at him. He looked like a biker with his leather vest and a big body with tattoos on his arms. His hair and full beard were now mostly grey.

"I wish. Just too busy to get away." Stone exchanged greetings with two other men he knew and was introduced to a middle-aged couple, Pete and Wendy.

Pete was slimly built, with a full head of hair. His wife was slightly heavier, her hair a dirty-blonde colour. She asked, "Stone, is that a real name or your nickname?"

"It's real enough."

She smiled at him. "I like it. It suits you."

The group talked about riding and a couple of unknown roads that were good for biking. After his second beer, Stone headed back on the road. This time, he followed Range Road 33 south until he reached the Yellowhead Highway, turning east.

Stone had every intention of using his ride to clear his head and think about nothing except the open road. However, first Cindy, a girlfriend of a few months, came to his thoughts. They had decided to keep their relationship light, even nonexclusive. However, despite his vow to break off with anyone who became too close to him, he was the one falling for her. Yet she hadn't indicated to him that she wanted a change in their status. He suspected she may have a drink with a male co-worker a couple of times and wasn't sure if that classified as being on a date or not.

It is odd how I've fallen into a trap by the rules of my own making. Perhaps I need to have a talk with her. He turned up the throttle of the bike. *Then there's Anya. She has given me signals and it's tempting. Too tempting.* He saw the flashing coloured lights in the left side mirror. The police car pulled behind him. *Damn. Even thinking about women gets me in trouble.*

———

MONDAYS, STONE CONSIDERED, ALWAYS ARRIVED TOO SOON. *THERE should be another day squeezed between Saturday and Sunday.* He yawned as he entered the office and slouched into his chair. He ignored the computer on the desk, refusing to consider he had reports to finish.

"How was your bike ride on the weekend? Where did you end up going?"

"It was great. I went out to Alberta Beach. Riding, beer, and a burger. It doesn't get much better than that." He took a drink of his coffee. "Yours?"

"It was interesting. Nothing special."

He raised his eyebrows. "I suspect there was more to your weekend that you're letting on. But I won't press for details."

Roberts didn't comment on his assertion. It was true that she did go dancing with a couple of girlfriends at a local bar, where a younger man made a serious play for her. But she was not going to explain that to him, or why she spurned his efforts. "What do we do next?"

"We need to find out more about our victim. I guess that means we need to interview family and other acquaintances besides his drinking buddies. I guess we start with his brothers and sister."

"Okay, I'll get their names and address."

They used the elevator to reach the basement where vehicles were parked and walked to his car when Roberts ventured another question. "Did you take Cindy with you?"

"No, she was busy. I did a solo trip."

"Just make sure you drive carefully. I don't ever want to hear that you ended up in the hospital after riding your bike. One moment of not paying attention and you could be toast."

He nodded. His moment of not paying attention and thinking about the women in his life resulted in him being pulled over. The woman, an RCMP officer, asked him why he was speeding, and without giving it much thought, told her his girlfriend was causing his mind to wander. "The more I thought of her, the faster my bike went," he explained at the time. The female cop laughed unexpectedly and let him off with a warning. "You just be careful what you're thinking about when you're driving, especially on a bike. Maybe save your thinking about women for when you're sitting at home."

5

JOHN CARLTON ANSWERED THE DOOR TO THE BUNGALOW. HE wasn't surprised to see the detectives, having received a courtesy call first to ensure he was home. He invited them into the well-appointed living room, where his wife, Sandra, brought in a tray of coffee and biscuits.

Roberts led the questioning. "We're sorry for your loss but we need to ask if you knew if Jacob had any enemies? Anyone who would like to see him dead?" She looked first at John, the oldest sibling, and then at his wife. Both looked passive, although John's face was turning red.

His jaws worked a few moments before words came out. "Jacob was always a rebel. Always speaking his mind. So, I guess he made a few enemies that way. The thing is he drifted away from us and the rest of the family. He wanted to prove how tough he could be. He drank too much. I don't know why he felt he needed to do what he did." John clasped his hands and looked at the floor.

Sandra added, breaking the silence, "I think some of the drugs Jacob took affected his brain, his way of thinking. He may have been an alcoholic, too."

"He was involved in an accident while driving?"

Sandra nodded. "He struck a pedestrian one afternoon. He already had a few drinks and didn't see the lights had changed. He escaped the charges with just a fine and a suspended licence."

"Was the family of the victim upset?"

"Well, obviously they would be. But as far as I know, they never acted hostile or demanded more than what the insurance paid them."

"When was the last time you had contact with Jacob?"

John had composed himself well enough to answer. "Four months ago. He called me to wish me a happy birthday." Tears rolled down his cheeks.

Sandra quickly spoke. "I don't believe we can help you with any answers. We just don't know more than what we've told you."

Stone asked, "Were any of the other siblings closer to him?"

"Simon, the youngest, was the only one who Jacob contacted occasionally. He would be the best one to see."

Roberts spoke as they left for his car. "I guess we should talk to Simon next. There sure are a lot of tears for a bad man."

"Hmm. I would say despite Jacob's unsocial behaviour, the family is otherwise very close."

Simon lived by himself in an apartment condo. Still single, he made a good living selling artwork to various galleries. Stone thought he looked like an artist; a striped shirt left open over a white T-shirt, worn jeans, and a scruffy beard. He wasn't big and displayed a relaxed attitude as he showed the two detectives into the living room.

"I suppose you're here to talk about Jacob."

"Yes," Stone replied. "We're sorry for your loss, but we need to ask some questions. Do you know if he had any enemies? Someone having a grudge strong enough to kill him?"

"I don't know. He was always short of money. I usually would give him a hundred bucks every few weeks. He called it a loan but I knew I'd never see the money again."

"What did he use the money for? Did he say?"

"Drugs. He never told me that but it wasn't hard to figure it out."

"Do you think he may have had a big debt that ended up getting him killed?"

Simon thought for a moment. "No. He would've come to me if he needed more money. I think he mouthed off to someone and that may have started a chain of events. Jacob never could restrain himself. Drugs, booze, and opinions. Mix those, and you have Jacob."

"You don't know anything specific that may have led to his demise?"

"No. He was a troubled man. Maybe he's finally at peace."

"Is it possible drugs caused his behaviour issues?"

"No, I don't think so. More like the other way around. His personality meant he craved the feeling of being high or drunk."

"He was involved in an accident that left someone severely injured. Any thoughts about that?"

For the first time an emotion showed on Simon's face. "I was really mad at him then. I told him it was his choice if he wanted to hurt his body by drinking and taking drugs but he had no right to hurt others because he decided it was okay to drive drunk. The sad thing is he had apologized, but I could tell he wasn't sincere and he'd drink and drive again."

Roberts commented after they left, "Our Jacob was not a very responsible man. I suspect he may have made one enemy too many. Now which one wanted to see him dead is another thing."

"Yeah, more digging into his past may reveal some more clues, but this is not an easy case."

"What's the next step? Or are you going to sleep on it?"

"More like drink on it. A couple of my buddies are getting together for beer and wings tonight."

"On a weekday night? Don't overdo it."

"Me overdo it? Never."

Her eyes narrowed. "Obviously you don't understand the term overdoing it."

6

ANYA ROBERTS PIVOTED ON HER FIVE-WHEEL CHAIR AS MOSS STONE entered the office, looking unenthusiastic about the day. She watched him trudge across the room to his desk, gripping his paper coffee cup as if it possessed life itself. She waited until he had plunked himself in his chair. Their desks faced each other and she had a clear view of him. *At least he shaved.*

"Where did you go last night?"

"Beer and wing night at Hooters." His reply was directed to his desk. He slowly eased the coffee cup to his mouth.

"Hooters, where the women walk around in shorts. I hope it was worth it."

"It was." He glanced at her eyes. "Good wings, good beer, and great service."

"I'm sure the girls are friendly there."

He sighed. "They are. Ever been there?"

She shook her head.

"Look, how about we have a few minutes of silence. I need this coffee more than conversation." He pulled the rest of the lid off, deciding the small tear-off portion of the lid was hindering the consumption of the black liquid. The effect of the caffeine didn't have an immediate effect, and he leaned back, taking a deep breath.

As he took a second gulp, Anya commented, "You remind me of a vampire, only instead of blood, you require coffee for sustenance."

"Coffee is better, less messy."

She opened her desk drawer. "Want a painkiller?"

"No, took a couple of Tylenol just before I got here. They should kick in soon enough. That and the coffee."

"Your lifeblood." She grinned, walked around the desk and placed a hand on his shoulder. "I'll get you another cup, and then we actually have to do some work."

———

STONE SQUINTED AT THE MONITOR SCREEN THAT SEEMED unusually bright. He finished his coffee, reviewing the details of the latest case he and Roberts were handed. As he finished the document, Roberts placed a new coffee on his desk.

"What do you think?" She peered over his shoulder.

He summarized what they had learned so far into the murder. "Let's see, a bar fight. A knife was used. Someone gets shot. No one admits to anything. Big surprise."

"Some video surveillance of the parking lot where the fight took place, but inside the bar we can see how the escalation started. The bouncer kicked them out and that's when the real trouble started."

"So, the fight starts in the bar and the bar throws them out all at the same time. How was that supposed to end okay?"

"Obviously it didn't."

Stone read aloud the report on the victim. "Gun wounds just below the rib cage on the right side led to rapid blood loss."

"Our basic bar fight gone wrong, except it happened blocks away from the bar. That means his murder may have not been related to the bar fight. Do you want to interview his sister? The brother we haven't interviewed lives in Vancouver and I doubt it's worthwhile doing anything more than a telephone interview."

"Sure, let's talk to his sister. I need to move around."

"I'll drive." She knew he preferred to drive, not liking how slow she drove, but his hangover prevented him from objecting.

"You are still seeing Cindy, aren't you? She didn't want to go with you last night?" Anya carefully pulled into traffic from the parking lot.

"Guys night out. Still seeing her, maybe not as much as before."

"Romance cooling off a bit?"

"No romance involved. We're just going out with each other. She's had a couple of extra shifts at The Craft Beer Market."

"Okay, that happens. She seems to have hung on a long time with you. I'll have to meet her sometime."

"Oh, no. You interviewing one of my girlfriends? No good could ever come out of that."

Roberts laughed. "I wouldn't interrogate her. I just would like to meet the girl that has such staying power."

"Right. Not going to happen. What about your dating life? What's going on there?"

"Nothing. That may be good or bad. Bad in that I don't have a companion, good in that I'm not dealing with any creeps."

"You have such a high opinion of men."

"Reality bites."

———

Jacob Carlton's sister, Angela McNider, was a slim, polite host. She apologized for the mess in her living room, although Stone failed to detect what might have been out of place. The room was large with big, comfortable chairs.

"My husband isn't home and the kids are over at a friend's place, so you've picked a good time to ask me about Jacob."

"Your husband didn't approve of Jacob?" Stone asked.

"Why do you say that?" McNider acted surprised.

"You said we picked a good time to talk to you and mentioned your husband wasn't home. I suspect he may have offered a harsher comment about Jacob than yourself."

She nodded. "Yes, Duggan didn't have any patience for Jacob's lifestyle. He didn't want him around our kids and didn't make him feel welcome at family functions."

"And why was that?"

"Jacob was an addict. Everyone could see that, except Mom and Dad." She gave a short smile. "The other thing was, even when he was a kid, he loved to debate and argue on just about everything. He once told our parents he was an atheist and I suspect he said that just to get an argument going." Suddenly, a tear broke free from her eye. She didn't do anything to stop its slide down her cheek. "He was so troubled, never at peace with himself or this world. I knew that someday I would hear he had been killed, either from a drug overdose or a bar fight. I thank God it wasn't by suicide."

"You feared he'd kill himself?"

"Yes. I know he felt guilty about the things he had done. Actually, his life in general. If he had killed himself, that would have devastated my parents and John." She paused. "They are quite religious and believe suicide is a sin that may prevent you from going to heaven."

"I understand." Stone waited as McNider finally used a tissue to dab at her eyes. "Are you aware of anyone who would plan to murder him? A gun was used, and it appeared it wasn't a robbery, but a planned event."

McNider gave a small gasp. "That is horrible that someone would hate him so. He was just troubled and never meant to hurt others."

"He did injure someone while drinking and driving." Stone raised his eyebrows.

More tears flowed. "Yes, that poor woman. Duggan and I visited her in the hospital. We wanted to see if there was anything we could do for her. We knew she was suing for a lot of money, as she was entitled to. We just wanted her to know our family wanted to show her our support and that we'd pray for her well-being."

"How did she react?"

"Very neutral. I guess she was surprised by our visit. In the end, she did thank us for our concern. Understandably, she was still in shock of being told of her diagnosis."

"She was alone at the time?"

"No, her sister was there. She didn't say anything but just glared at us.

I can't blame her. We were Jacob's family and represented the man who did this awful thing."

"Do you recall the sister's name?"

"No. I'm not sure if we were introduced. She wasn't big and had an intense look on her face."

Stone and Roberts thanked her for her time.

She started her car and asked, "Where to now?"

"How about that corner store we passed earlier. I need something to drink."

Roberts laughed. "Still paying the price for your beer and wing night?"

"Not entirely. I missed breakfast and now feeling I need to fuel up a bit."

When they stopped at the convenience store, she accepted his offer to bring her back a drink as well. A few minutes later, he returned with two plastic bottles of flavoured water and an energy bar. As he took a bite of the bar, his phone chirped. "Damn." He fumbled with the phone in his left hand and hit the answer button and then the speakerphone mode. He placed the phone on the dash.

"Stone here."

"Detective Stone, this is Roberta Constantino of the RCMP. We met a few days ago on Highway Sixteen."

Stone saw Roberts give him a look that meant there would be questions afterward. He suddenly wished the conversation was private.

7

McNab was the last to show up at the small theatre located in the new wing of Grant McEwan campus. It was a bit of a distance from his office and he had to push past the slow moving crowd in the hallways. He was annoyed he had forgotten about the time and now cursed the students blocking his way.

He quickly made his way to the front of the stage area.

"Okay, positions everyone. Let's start where Karrie pushes Nicholas onto the couch and then move on to our scene in the kitchen." McNab clapped his hands. "Dana, would you lead with the line 'I wasn't lost. I just had to park so damn far away'."

The small theatre inside the McEwan campus made for a convenient spot for most of the actors to rehearse the play.

Dana Sharpe closed her eyes momentarily and stepped toward where Mitch Donnelly stood near Brenda Thompson. She held a red plastic cup that represented a can of beer used in the play.

"I wasn't lost. I just had to park so damn far away." She pretended to drink from the cup. "That tastes good."

Mitch Donnelly frowned slightly and responded. "Hi, Karrie. It's good to see you."

Sharpe looked at him up and down. "Well, cowboy. It's good seeing you, too." She tapped her plastic cup against a similar one he was holding. "Cheers."

Donnelly reacted by pretending to take a drink from his plastic cup. "Cheers."

Thompson touched Donnelly on the arm. "Why don't you two get reacquainted? I want to show Jon some of my lecture notes. I have a question about something." She walked off the immediate stage area and stood slightly behind McNab.

Sharpe paused a moment before speaking. "You know, I was hoping we would be able to get together sometime." She grabbed Donnelly's shirt in one hand, pulling him close. "I think Terri is right, and we should get re-acquainted." Sharpe hesitated and quickly kissed Donnelly.

Donnelly dropped his plastic cup and kissed Sharpe in return. His return kiss was more aggressive than hers and she took a step back.

She quickly recovered and returned to her memorized dialogue. "Come on, cowboy. Let's make use of our alone time here." She placed a hand on Donnelly's chest and pushed him toward the couch. Donnelly fell on his back on the cushions and Sharpe sat on top of him. She placed a hand on his shoulder and lowered herself slightly. Sharpe looked at McNab and appeared to be relieved when he clapped his hands once.

"Okay, let's now go on to the kitchen scene." He spoke to Sharpe and Donnelly. "I need to see more emotion from both of you on our next rehearsal. You spoke the lines flat and your body language was too stiff. You're supposed to feel excited about having time together." He pointed at Tyler and Brenda. "Now that was a nice show of affection between you. That's what I want to see. If the script is for you to be lovers, then you need to act that way toward each other." He pointed at Paul Church and Tanya Conner. "Okay, start with 'See, I know where the wine is kept'."

Donnelly watched the scene from the couch. He was glad Sharpe quickly got up from sitting on him. He wasn't especially fond of her, finding her too skinny for his liking. It was also apparent she didn't enjoy kissing him and he felt annoyance that she thought he wasn't up to her standards. His feelings toward Sharpe were nothing compared to his anger at Church and Conner. The scene required them to kiss and make out, but as he sat clutching his fists, he could tell they weren't just acting. "That son-of-a-bitch." He muttered under his breath.

"Louder," McNab called out. "The audience needs to hear your words. This is not a time for soft voices."

Donnelly stood, taking slow breaths. He saw how Church pretended to open her top. In the actual play, her top would be open, and she would be exposed to him. Even though she indicated she would wear a camisole underneath her blouse, the thought irritated him. Church picked Conner easily up at the waist and sat her on the table, climbing on top of the surface as well.

"Okay, excellent. That's was good, not perfect by any means, but a step toward what we need to be to the play." McNab used his hands to indicate the cast to gather around him. "Now, I want everyone to remember that you need to *project* your voice. This is important..."

Donnelly was barely listening, seething at Church. *That asshole first takes my role, and now, he's trying to take my girl. Not going to happen.*

———

CONNER STOOD CLOSE TO CHURCH AS MCNAB SPOKE ABOUT THE need to speak louder. She made sure their arms touched and felt excited about their scene. Then she saw Donnelly, and his glare caused her to want to take a half step back. *Oh shit. He looks mad. Well, tough luck, Mitch. I've found a new man.*

McNab finished his lecture, urging the actors to study their lines and reminding them of the time of the next rehearsal.

Conner watched Donnelly quickly make his way toward her.

"That was one fucking performance," Donnelly snarled. He forced himself between Church and Conner. "Let's go." He grabbed her wrist and began to pull her off the stage.

"Hey!" Church hurried after them.

Conner held up her hand. "It's okay. I'll call you later." She went with Donnelly, looking back at the shocked expressions of the others on stage.

"Mitch, let go of me. You're hurting me."

He pushed open the exit door. "What the hell is going on? That was no fucking acting. You were enjoying kissing him. What kind of shit is this?"

She tugged her arm free and walked with him after they exited the room. "Okay, let's talk." When he didn't say anything, she continued. "I'm sorry, but it's over between us. And it's not just because of Paul. You were treating me like an annoyance for weeks. I'm gone and you should be happy about that."

"Fuck it and fuck him. He better hope I don't find him alone." He stomped away.

Conner stopped, watching him disappear into the crowd. *Good riddance.*

———

DANA SHARPE WAS SHOCKED AT HOW DONNELLY HAD MARCHED Conner out of the room. She had thought someone would have moved to help her, in particular, Church. *He certainly was the cause of Mitch's jealousy. He should've stepped in but it's obviously not in his DNA to do the right thing.*

Sharpe exited the theatre and made her way to where a collection of vending machines stood behind a few chairs and tables. She dropped a few coins into a machine, and seconds later, a bottle of diet cola appeared. She sat at a table, wondering if she should remain in the play or if it would be better if she quit. *McNab will be upset if I quit but that's not my problem. He's such a pompous twit anyway.* She sat, thinking. Then a couple went by, Church and Conner, talking in, what seemed to Sharpe, excited dialogue with much hand gesturing. Church was doing most of the talking and by the time they had passed the vending machine and tables, Conner had moved closer to Church. He responded by putting his arm around her.

Well, I guess Paul came out ahead on this confrontation. He lives a charmed life. Well, so far anyway.

8

"Yes, Corporal Constantino, I recall meeting you." Stone tried to keep his voice professional, hoping she wasn't going to ask him anything personal.

"I was surprised when I contacted your homicide division and was given your name to help us out with a murder inquiry. It was a bit of a coincidence."

He could hear the hint of amusement in her voice. He almost replied that there weren't any coincidences, but decided not to push his philosophy. "What kind of murder inquiry?"

"A Travis Moore was murdered on the same day last Saturday, that is the same day we met, in his home in Stony Plain. It turns out he had just recently moved to Stony Plain from Edmonton, so I was checking to see if he had any history with the local police."

"Okay, I'll do a background check. You said he was murdered last Saturday? And you just discovered his body?"

"We received a distraught call yesterday and are now just following up on leads. Do you have time to get together? I'd like to hear your thoughts on the case. It seems you have an excellent reputation for solving cases."

———

Roberts launched a barrage of questions after the phone conversation ended. "She sounded like she likes you. Why and how did you meet her? What does she look like? Do you think she only wants to meet you about a murder case?"

Stone rolled his eyes. "Good Lord, crank down the inquisition."

"Then talk."

"I met her because I was speeding on my way back from my trip to Alberta Beach. She stopped me and just gave me a warning. End of story."

"End of story? I don't think so."

"What you think is not going to get me to talk any more about this."

"Really? I have my ways to get you to talk." She gave him a grin.

———

Peter McNab sat in his office, going over the day's events. He hadn't expected to have problems in his troupe. He knew there could be personality problems among actors, but he didn't foresee what had transpired today. McNab blamed Church for the situation, deciding he had taken advantage of Conner. *He shouldn't be taking advantage of women in the play. I hope nothing else goes wrong.*

9

Stone and Roberts walked into the pizza restaurant at the appointed time. Boston Pizza, located in Mayfield Common, was doing a lively business at lunchtime. Roberts and Stone didn't receive undue attention when they walked through the dining room, spotting Corporal Roberta Constantino at one of the back booths. Stone suspected she received more attention on her stroll past the tables since she was wearing an RCMP uniform.

She gave them a warm smile as they approached.

"Well, Detective Stone, you do clean up well. Quite a change from your motorbike persona."

Stone laughed. "My alter ego. This is Anya Roberts, my partner."

Constantino looked between Roberts and Stone several times. She appeared to want to say something, stopped, and merely acknowledged Roberts. "Good to meet you, Anya."

Roberts guessed Constantino was speculating on to what extent Stone and she were partners. "So, you were the one who pulled Moss over for speeding."

"Yeah. I had a good quota of tickets issued already, so I decided to let him off after he gave an excuse of thinking too much about women."

Roberts laughed. "He does have problems with women."

Stone held up a hand. "How about we talk about the reason why we're here. Murder case. Does that ring any bells?"

Roberts smiled at Constantino. "But it's so much more fun making Moss feel uncomfortable."

Stone sighed as the two women laughed.

Constantino turned serious. "All right. I really do need some help on this. My first murder investigation, so I could use your help on how to approach this. The murder occurred in a house near the downtown area of Stony Plain. Travis Moore was renting the house but was previously from Edmonton. He had been living in Stony Plain for a couple of months."

Stone slid a folder over to Constantino. "This is his criminal record. Disorderly conduct, speeding tickets, drinking and driving on more than one occasion. He has a suspended licence. He was convicted of a hit and run of a pedestrian, who later died."

Constantino read out loud from the report. "He wasn't charged with drinking and driving that time. I'm guessing by the time they found him, it was too late to measure the alcohol content in his blood. Still, he served three months in jail and lost his licence for a year."

"Not much time for killing someone," Roberts commented.

Constantino shrugged. "It's our justice system." She paused as the server took their orders and then resumed speaking to Roberts and Stone. "Judging by his police record, he may have made a few enemies. It could be that he got into an altercation in his house that resulted in his death."

"How did he die?" Stone inquired.

"Blunt force trauma to the head. It wasn't a pretty sight. Several blows and lots of blood loss."

"Any murder weapon found?"

"No. And there wasn't any sign of forced entry either. We are working on the assumption he knew his killer."

Stone took a drink of his coffee. "How big was Moore? What kind of condition was he in physically?"

"He was fifty-four years old. Slim, very slim build, maybe one hundred and fifty pounds. He stood five foot nine."

"Any signs of defensive wounds?"

"There were marks on one hand. None on his arms."

Stone continued with his questions. "When did the death occur? Who discovered his body?"

"A friend of his, Brian Greenly. Greenly was quite upset about discovering the body, as you might expect. They were going to Edmonton to go to Costco. Since Moore didn't have a licence, Greenly offered to take him. From what I gather, Greenly and Moore were mere acquaintances, not drinking buddies. They were supposed to get together just before lunchtime, and Moore was going to buy him lunch at the River Cree Casino. We're tentatively putting the time of death sometime after nine a.m." Constantino waited as their lunch was placed on the table. "I'm checking the local bars to see if he was in any arguments the night before, but so far I don't have any suspects."

"Fair enough. Judging by what you said that there were multiple blows to the head, this wasn't just an argument gone to an extreme. Someone meant to kill him. If it happened in the morning, then it wasn't on impulse after a few drinks."

"That's a good point. More like someone planned to kill him."

"With the type of attack you mentioned, and a large amount of blood loss, I would expect the killer would have blood spatters on their clothing."

"There was also a spot on the floor where the killer stepped on some of the blood."

"That will help when you find a suspect. You can check their clothing and the bottom of the shoes for evidence of blood. As for finding a suspect, I have a suggestion. You may want to canvass the surrounding neighbourhood if there were any vehicles parked that don't belong to anyone living there. If the killer made a visit to Moore with the intention to kill him, then they would not have wanted to have parked in front of his house. Too easy for a witness to make note of the vehicle. The killer may have parked a block or two away."

At the end of the lunch, Stone insisted on paying for it, telling Constantino he owed her a favour for letting him off on a speeding ticket.

She laughed. "That's all right. Just stop thinking about women when you drive."

———

ROBERTS BUCKLED HER SEAT BELT AND COMMENTED, "SHE SEEMED nice."

"Yeah, she's all right. Easy to talk to."

"What did she mean by don't think about women while driving? Exactly which women were you thinking about?"

"Just a joke. I told her I was speeding because I was thinking of my girlfriend."

She decided not to press for more information. *But Roberta did say, women, as in plural. Does that mean anything?* "Are we going to go back to work on our own murder investigation now?"

"Yeah. Carlton's cell phone had some information we can work with, like his recent contacts."

"Probably a lovely crowd."

"No doubt."

Roberts opened the file and saw the list of names associated with phone numbers located on Carlton's cell. "I know one of these names."

"Really? How?"

"My cousin."

"Your cousin?"

"Yeah, Ben Thomason," Roberts replied. "He does real estate. He never married but lives common-law with Chantelle. Two kids." She frowned.

"The black sheep of the family?"

"I suppose so. They seem nice enough, but Ben is so full of himself. Acts a bit immature. Drinks too much at family get-togethers. Chantelle used to be an exotic dancer."

"A stripper?" Stone peered at Roberts with renewed interest.

"She prefers the term exotic dancer and isn't shy about letting people know of her past." She looked back at him. "Maybe you'll recognize her."

He laughed. "Maybe I will. I have to admit, I did have a wild past."

"Just your past?"

"I'm a saint compared to what I used to be."

"I'll let the pope know of your new status."

———

THE HOME OF BEN THOMASON AND CHANTELLE DAWSON WAS A newish two-story home on the south side of Edmonton. Roberts had phoned ahead of time to let Thomason know they were coming over. As soon as Stone's car stopped in front of the home, Thomason stepped outside of the house.

Stone looked up at him as he stood on the front steps. Tall with dark hair, he wore dress pants and shirt.

"Anya, how are you doing?" He went down the concrete steps and met them halfway to the house.

"I'm fine. This is Moss Stone." She indicated Stone with her hand and waited as Thomason shook his hand. "We're investigating the death of Jacob Carlton."

"Jacob Carlton?" He sounded puzzled at first, then acknowledged the name. "I do know a Jacob but not his last name."

Stone responded. "This Jacob knew you. He had your cell number in his phone."

"Yeah. Look, I only know him because I bought some pot from him. Just the odd time."

Stone noticed a blonde woman standing by the door, her features partially obscured by the screen door. "How often did you buy from him?"

"Hmm, maybe four, six, seven times."

Stone raised his eyebrows. "Counting isn't your strong suit, I take it. When was the last time you spoke to or saw Jacob? I need you to be a little more exact on this question." He saw the woman had stepped outside and was approaching them. Her face was without expression.

Thomason pulled his large cell phone from his pocket and checked the screen. After a few moments, he answered, "Fifteen days ago I texted him I needed some pot. Two days later I met him, and I paid him for a bag."

The blonde looked at Roberts and Stone. "What's going on here?"

Thomason replied, "Honey, this is the police. They're investigating the death of the guy I buy pot from."

She crossed her arms. "Well, he certainly didn't have anything to do with that."

Stone studied the woman wearing blue jean shorts and a fitted sleeveless green top. He speculated she may have gained a bit of weight since her dancing days but still was a looker.

"We're not saying he did, but he may have information about the victim." He turned his attention back to Thomason. "What time did you meet and where?"

"It was in the afternoon, in the parking lot of the Dragonhead's Bar. I met him in the bar, had a beer, and then we went outside for a smoke. We did our business there."

Dawson interrupted. "I better go and check on the kids." She walked back to the house.

Stone noticed her walk was that of a woman expected to be watched coming and going. "Why in the parking lot and not inside the bar?"

"The manager of the bar gets upset if he sees anyone doing drug sales inside the bar. If he sees you do it, then you're banned."

"Okay, so you only bought, not sold?"

"Right."

"Why him? How did you meet him?"

"I was in the bar one night and saw him. He looked like a guy who sold stuff, so I bought a small amount. His price was average and it was good quality, so I went to him afterward."

"Was he with anyone anytime you saw him?"

"No, I think he was pretty much alone. Mind you, I usually met him in the parking lot or outside somewhere. So, if he was with anyone, they were probably waiting for him inside the bar."

"Okay, that's it for now. Thanks for your time, Mr. Thomason."

"Anya, what's going to happen now? Is my name going to come out on this?"

"If you told us everything, then this may be it. Look, I'm not going to lecture you and Chantelle on smoking pot, but you better not start using harder stuff. You're responsible for the well-being of your kids, Daniele and Katie. Don't screw up because you feel the need to escape reality."

He nodded. "I promise."

Stone spoke as they drove off. "He seems okay."

"He's all right. He makes good money but spends it on stupid stuff. Like he owns a big boat that he maybe uses twice a year."

"It's their money. She doesn't work?"

"No. Stay-home mom."

"Good for her. She's still good-looking."

"Yeah, she works out a lot. I assume you didn't recognize her from her past stage performances."

"No, she kept her clothes on."

10

McNab flipped through his manuscript once again. His office at Grant McEwan was the standard size for teaching professors but looked smaller. The walls were covered with posters from his favourite plays. Some of the posters were partially obscured by the stacks of cardboard boxes and papers. A few metal folding chairs were stored against the wall near the door, used when his office became a meeting spot. His wood desk was littered with notes, paper, and various ceramic cups. The cups held different amounts of tea, and he sometimes inadvertently drank from one of the room-temperature liquids, rather than a hot one he just prepared.

He put down the script, wondering if he needed to change part of the dialogue and action between two of the characters when a knock on his open door interrupted him. McNab looked up, seeing Dana Sharpe. "Yes, Dana?" He noticed her reserved expression. "Is there a problem?"

She stepped into his office. "I'm sorry, but I have to withdraw from the play."

"You do? What happened? Is it due to the incident in the play involving Paul? If so, I can assure you I plan to make sure there won't be a repeat of such unprofessional behaviour."

Dana hesitated a moment and shook her head. "No, it's not just that.

Something has come up. A family problem. I have to go to Red Deer and help my sister. Sorry."

McNab let out a sigh. "Very well. I guess I'll have to find someone else to take over your role. I'll check to see if anyone else from the class is available. Unfortunately, with our Live Theatre classes finished, most will be hard to get a hold of."

"Why not ask Jessica? She has acting experience."

"An excellent suggestion. I shall contact her immediately."

"Good luck with the play. If things work out with my sister, I'll try to come down and watch the play later."

As soon as Sharpe left, McNab called Jessica Knowles on her mobile. He was surprised when she answered almost immediately and he stumbled out a hello.

"Jessica, this is Professor Peter McNab, well, just Peter. I..." He quickly composed himself and made his request. He was pleased she was at the university campus and agreed to come by his office to discuss a change in the play. He felt embarrassed how he first spoke with her, wanting to believe his voice alone could inspire respect from those around him.

McNab thought of himself as an unrealized genius when it came to playwriting. His previous works had been either ignored or rejected. He had decided that if Hollywood and Broadway didn't appreciate his scripts and plays yet, he would turn to a local venue to win praise. The Fringe would be his chance to spring into the limelight. Even though it was only a local play, he was sure those in larger centres would take notice and the steps to success would begin.

"Peter." Jessica Knowles tapped on the doorframe and entered the small space in front of his desk. She smiled with perfect white teeth showing. "You wanted to see me?"

"Yes, yes." McNab suddenly felt warm. Knowles's loose top and short skirt gave him pause. He attempted to recover. "We have a situation suddenly thrust upon us, that is the play. Dana has a family situation and has withdrawn from the play. I immediately considered that you, since you're already familiar with the play, could step in and take over the part of Karrie. Besides being the stage manager, that is if you don't think that's too much."

"Peter, I'd love to step in and do some acting. I'll study the lines. It shouldn't be a problem to also be the stage manager. Thank you for thinking of me." She waltzed out of the office after saying goodbye.

McNab stared at the empty doorway for a few seconds and then returned to the work on his desk. Initially, he was upset when Dana Sharpe suddenly withdrew from the play, citing a family matter as an excuse. Her suggestion of using Knowles as a replacement made him feel better, especially when Knowles readily agreed.

Now, he pondered what else could be done in the play. A small change in wording or action could occasionally make a play stand out, become real to the audience. He mouthed each line and gestured with his hands as he moved through his play. He placed his hand on his chin, nodded, and swiveled in his chair to turn on his computer. He loathed the device sitting on his desk, preferring pen and paper to the keyboard and LCD screen. He also stored paper records rather than use the memory on the computer. He thought of the Apple computer slightly less evil than Microsoft and grudgingly used it to make up revisions on the play.

As he heard the printer spew out the revised play, he leaned back in his chair. He could envision the interview of the eccentric professor in the newspaper, one who stared down the modern convenience of computers. One who only drank tea, not coffee. A confirmed vegan who thought the world was going to collapse under its own garbage. His ex would be so annoyed reading about his triumph.

McNab left his office, ensuring the door was locked behind him. He made his way down the corridor, not as busy as with the daytime students but now filling with those taking evening classes. A voice behind him called out.

"Professor McNab?"

He spun around, recognizing a former student he taught last year. "Marc Crestman."

"Yes, I thought I'd say hello."

McNab liked Crestman, who did have what he considered some acting skill. The tall man had a fair appearance, and McNab now realized he would've made a good leading man for his play. *Unfortunately, it's likely too late to do anything about that now.* "It's good to see you, Marc. Are you taking evening classes?"

"Yeah, nothing exciting. I miss your acting classes though."

"Thank you. As you may be aware, I have written a play that is being featured at the Fringe. If you give me your mobile number, I'll arrange for you to be my guest at one of the performances."

"I would like that very much."

McNab said goodbye to his former student after taking his number. Quietly, he scolded himself for not having contacted Marc earlier for his play.

Carrying the precious sheets of paper in a leather attaché case, he hurried through a downpour to his Toyota Prius. He pretended to like his ecology friendly car but, in fact, was frustrated by the lack of creature comforts that were found in the vehicles his colleagues drove. Still, it did take him efficiently to his restored home near the University of Alberta campus, where a glass of scotch would soothe him. He was still slightly annoyed at Sharpe for dropping out of the play, for he was not one who enjoyed surprises. *If anyone else starts to sabotage my play, they will feel my full wrath and what I'm capable of. And that most certainly includes you, Mr. Church. Keep your romantic desires out of my play.*

11

PAUL CHURCH TOGGLED THE CONTROLS RAPIDLY AS HE WATCHED the screen intently. He mumbled to himself as the sound of explosions reached his ears.

Tanya Conner watched the action on the TV as she slouched on the couch next to him. "How much longer? We're supposed to meet Janet soon."

He grunted. "Okay, I'll save the game. Got to another level anyway."

She reached over and poked him in his ribs. "Good. Get a shirt on and let's get out of here."

He pressed a few more buttons on the control, shut off the TV, stretched, and stood. She watched him wander to his bedroom. She liked how he always stayed calm, even when Donnelly was making a situation difficult with an aggressive stance. That calmness also meant he wasn't concerned about time. She tried to remain patient as he sauntered out of the bedroom, buttoning up a green patterned shirt. "You know I don't like being late." She gave him a smile. Their relationship was too new for her to be making demands.

"The world won't end if she gets there before us." His arm swung around her waist. "But if you want, we can run there instead of walking." He locked the wood door as she went ahead of him on the stairs. "Oh sure. Heels on my shoes and a bra that would bounce off on the second step. No thank you." She laughed as she took his hand.

Church wondered why she was anxious about meeting her friend. First, the worry about being late. At most, they would only be two or three minutes late. Then, there was the extra effort she spent in the washroom with her hair. Finally, he was surprised she kept on the high heels she had on last night rather than the flat shoes she had in her overnight bag.

"So, what is your friend like? I take it you haven't seen her for a while."

"It's been a few months. She went to New Zealand for a working holiday. She's back here for a short visit."

They crossed 124th Street to walk on the west sidewalk, heading north. She liked the shops along the street but didn't want to spend time window shopping. As they approached their destination, Church commented, "You said you've known her a long time and that she used to live in Edmonton. She's here by herself? She didn't bring a boyfriend on her trip?"

Conner was silent for a few seconds. "As far as I know, she doesn't have a partner." Then another, longer pause. "She's into women, not men."

"Okay." He opened the door to The Duchess Bakery, letting her enter first. "Hey, just how good a friend were you with her?" He grinned at his joke and then saw her blush. A woman, tall, slim, and wearing black pants and an expensive-looking T-shirt stood at a table, waving at them or, more specifically, at Conner.

Conner hurried over and gave her a hug and a quick kiss on the cheek. Church slowly made his way over, and after introducing himself, shook Janet's hand.

"Janet Gourneau."

"You ladies catch up. I'll order some pastry and coffee. What would you like, Janet?"

Gourneau smiled. "A black Americano, if you don't mind."

He looked at Conner. "Cappuccino?"

"Yes, please." She reached for her purse.

"No, it's on me."

After they sat down and Church had made his way to the counter, Conner asked, "So when did you get into Edmonton?"

"My plane landed yesterday. You were the first person I called. I couldn't wait to see you."

"I was so excited to hear your voice. How long are you going to be here?"

"Not long. I'm just on vacation, so I have to return to work in a couple of weeks."

"We'll have to use that time to catch up a bit. Hey, I'm in a play at the Fringe. I can get you a ticket to see it."

"I'd love that."

————

CHURCH ENTERED THE LINE THAT WENT PAST THE GLASS DISPLAYS of delicious-looking pastries. He glanced back at the women, both were talking at the same time, and each had a hand on the table where their fingertips touched.

He carried the pastries back to the table, an assortment of a few he found of interest. "They'll call when the coffee is ready." He sat next to Conner and looked at Janet, who was peering at him intently. "Well, are you two catching up?"

Conner smiled and withdrew her hand from the table. "I think we have established where we are now."

Church nodded. "Tanya tells me you two were friends before and you moved to New Zealand."

Gourneau replied, "Oh, we never stopped being friends. We stayed close, even when I was far away. Tanya and I have...a connection." She laughed, and moments later, Conner joined her with a giggle.

Conner added, "Janet is going to see our play. She said she never knew I was into acting and is excited to watch us perform." She turned her attention back to Gourneau, "I have to warn you though. The play is adult orientated. Paul actually rips open my top and places me on a table before kissing me."

"Now that may be worth the price of the ticket alone." Gourneau looked at Church with a hard smile. "Is that how you met?"

He nodded. "It was easy to like her after the kissing scene."

"I should hope so." After the coffee was consumed, Gourneau looked at her cell phone. "I have to be going. But I'm going to be in town for a couple of weeks, so we'll have to do a girls' night." She stood. "Nice meeting you, Paul." She went around the table and gave Conner a long hug and then a quick kiss on the cheek.

———

Church walked with Conner back to his apartment. "Would I be wrong to think Janet wants to re-establish a close relationship with you?"

"I know how it looks. My former girlfriend, okay, partner, wants to get back together with me. But I told her I've changed since she moved to New Zealand and that I'm with you. I really like being with you, Paul. She's not going to pull me away from you. I met her when I was vulnerable after I broke up with a guy I had been with over a year. She was strong and I just wanted someone to hold me, to care for me. So she really helped me in the past and I have feelings for her. But I told her that you're the one for me now. Okay?"

"Okay." He put his arm around her. "Thanks for letting me know. You don't owe me an explanation but I was kind of wondering where I stood."

"Next to me. That's where you stand."

12

MITCH DONNELLY GULPED HALF OF HIS BEER FROM THE PLASTIC cup. "Man, that tastes good right now." He sat next to his new girlfriend, Kimi, and across from another couple. He enjoyed being outside drinking beer, not caring it was a crowded location. The temporary beer garden was run by the Fringe festival in a parking lot, near where most of the plays were set up. The Fringe used various venues to host the plays. Smaller plays were done in bars and lounges. The smaller plays didn't usually require a large stage area, and usually the crowds could be better accommodated in the local bars. Some of the larger bars, such as the Cook County Saloon, could host larger performances as well. The plays that required a larger stage and higher seating capacity were held in venues designed for theatre, such as the Walterdale Theatre. The Walterdale Theatre was the location for *Death of a Philanderer*.

Donnelly kept his sunglasses on as protection from the afternoon sun, although the beer-themed table umbrellas provided some shade. He readjusted his hat and eyed a girl as she walked by. He knew others thought him a jerk and he didn't mind playing that role. For reasons he didn't worry about, being a rebel and owning a bike seemed to attract a lot of women. The fact was when he used to be a clean-cut guy, getting honours in school didn't do much for his social life. Now, he enjoyed the rush he received when he acted like a nonconformist. He still did well in his university courses, but few people knew that he was studying business and accounting.

Kimi Philips laughed. "Hot days will do that, along with working that play." She gave him a quick squeeze on his arm as she leaned into him.

Ralph and Marina, sitting across from them, raised their own beer cups. Ralph said, "To Mitch, on his excellent acting skills." He did his best to sound sincere, despite having seen the opening of the play earlier.

They all took a drink of their beer. Marina and Kimi sipped theirs, but Donnelly nearly finished his. Ralph stood as he eyed the near-empty cup. "I think that beer tasted like we need another. I'll get another round."

Ralph made his way through the noisy crowd to where the beer was dispensed. Approaching middle age, he made a successful living running a flooring store. He could blend into a crowd but had a quick smile and an easy disposition. He wondered what Kimi saw in Mitch. *That man is definitely anti-social. I sure wouldn't have him date my daughter. Who knows what he's capable of.* Ralph put four tickets on the counter for the smiling girl wearing a tight T-shirt and short shorts. He watched her retrieve the four cans of beer, glad the warm weather had influenced the way women dressed at the annual Edmonton International Fringe Festival. He helped her open each can and pour the contents into the plastic cups. "I'd prefer to drink it out of the can than these cups."

"I know, but we have to use cups. Liquor laws." She continued to smile as he dropped a couple of coins into the tip jar.

Ralph returned with the four beers, receiving thanks from everyone.

Kimi asked, "So there's just one more performance today?" The small redhead wore a bikini top under a tank top that helped emphasise her assets. Her shorts were loose and low slung and coupled with her top attracted a bit of attention. She was happy at Donnelly's sudden interest in her, having met him a month ago in a bar. A week ago, he contacted her and they spent considerable time in each other's company. She touched his arm again between sips of her beer.

"Yeah, one more." He took another gulp of beer. He could handle alcohol better than most, partly due to his lifestyle of partying that gave him a higher tolerance. He was considered attractive by those who liked men with slightly unkempt dark hair and a two-day beard and had a preference for colourful language. He wasn't overly tall but liked to wear heavy biker boots that gave him more stature.

"I'm looking forward to the next performance. I think *Death of a Philanderer* is one of the best plays at the Fringe." Kimi had seen only one other of the live plays but based her appraisal on the reviews done by the two major papers. The Edmonton Fringe Festival, the oldest and largest Fringe festival in North America, featured over two hundred plays for ten days starting in the middle of August. The theatres were spread out over five blocks in Old Strathcona, an area of Edmonton containing turn-of-the-century buildings. *Death of a Philanderer* was given a three-and-a-half-star rating and mostly positive Twitter comments.

———

MARINA WATCHED KIMI'S INTERACTION WITH DONNELLY. TALL with a runner's build, Marina wasn't surprised the two were together, surmising they suited each other. She did like him, knowing him from the neighbourhood where she grew up but had also seen the less-inspiring side of him. She was older by several years and remembered a few confrontations she had with him before he learned she didn't accept certain behaviours from him. Her easygoing Jamaican roots could flip around quickly when pushed. Marina hoped Kimi had her eyes open about him and suspected she knew exactly what type of person Donnelly was. From what she understood, he had been going out with Tanya Conner, an actress in the same play, and suddenly they were no longer an item. The rumour she heard was that it wasn't his decision and he didn't take disappointments well.

Donnelly finished his beer. "I gotta go. We have to go over some parts of the play. McNab didn't like something." He grunted as he stood. "Maybe something Paul did, fucking asshole."

"Do you want me to come along?" Kimi stood.

He shook his head. "This is just for those in the play." He stomped past the tables to the exit.

Marina looked at Kimi as she slowly sat. "Actors can be a bit moody at times." She gave a smile at the girl, trying to make her feel better. But she wondered why Donnelly couldn't have at least given her a quick kiss or promise to call her soon. He, in her opinion, treated his women poorly and took them for granted.

"I know. But they're meeting in a bar. I could've just hung out there until they were finished." She shrugged.

Ralph added, "You know, maybe Mitch thought it was going to be a long discussion and just didn't want you to have to wait around."

"I suppose so." She didn't sound convinced.

Marina finished her beer. "I've had enough to drink. Why don't we walk around?"

———

Donnelly reached Gateway Boulevard, also known as 103rd Street, and turned left to head south. He passed the El Cortez restaurant, where another smaller play was being held in the basement. The bar, like many of the others in the area, had a history of different owners. Some of the drinking establishments were at one time retail outlets or other types of businesses. The common theme in many of the bars and restaurants was character. Few trendy-looking bars were located in Old Strathcona, unless mismatched furniture and old brick walls could be identified as being trendy.

He pushed his way past the slow-moving crowd, absorbing the odour of cigarette smoke and beer. He crossed Whyte Avenue and turned right, walking two blocks to cross 105th Street. The walk didn't put him in a better frame of mind. When Conner rejected him for Church, it brought back memories of when as a quiet kid, too many girls ignored him for the taller boys. He found that if he wanted to get respect, he better be willing to fight for it. That meant acting like he was tougher than he was. There were some incidents that challenged his resolve, such as Marina threating to slap him silly if he did anything to her home. In the end, he emerged as an insecure kid with a false bravado intact. The crowded sidewalk caused him to curse as he went past the sluggish groups. He reached his destination, an old post office building. Downstairs, an Italian restaurant, Chianti, did a brisk business. Donnelly took the stairs to the second level to the bar. Inside, just past a set of doors, he climbed the wooden steps and looked around. Most of the tables had occupants around them, and the nearby pool tables provided a constant clicking sound as the balls were being hit. He saw McNab wave at him from across the room and headed over. There, a pair of tables were joined together, and he picked out one of the empty chairs, ignoring the one next to Conner. She gave him a long glance before returning her attention to her rum and cola.

Peter McNab announced the reason for the meeting. "Couple of things. First, we managed to make it through our first plays without a major mistake. I want to thank Jessica for stepping in on short notice to take over Dana's role and still handle the duties of a stage manager. Dana had a family emergency, but as we all know, the show must go on." He gave a thin smile that failed to inspire much confidence.

"The other thing is we need to express our characters' emotions better. You're not just reading lines; you need to express them as thoughts as well. I know we've rehearsed our lines, but now it's time to show your character's identity. Okay?" He looked at each person, getting nods or verbal assurance. "I know there are some conflicts here among us, but we need to focus on the play. We need to become the characters in the play. If the situation deteriorates, I will make changes. I will not have personal issues ruin my play."

Tyler Burgess snorted. "Don't you mean our play? Are we not all in this together?" He had little use for McNab, who he considered to be a pompous ass. Burgess, being the oldest member of the troupe, thought he could say what the others were thinking but were too intimidated by the professor to say. He didn't regret choosing to join McNab's group. Although he did rely on the fact McNab was an instructor at Grant McEwan College in performing arts who would take the play closer to a professional level, that turned out to be far from reality. But the murder-mystery play aspect appealed to him.

McNab's face reddened slightly. "Of course, I misspoke. All I ask is that we all make a serious commitment to the play and leave personal issues out of it."

———

CONNER GLANCED AT DONNELLY AND, NOT RECEIVING A LOOK IN return, briefly touched Church's arm. She was annoyed she had put herself in this awkward position. She knew she should have just broken it off with Donnelly and waited until the Fringe was over before making her feelings for Church known. But when the tall, well-mannered male lead kissed her, she suddenly found she couldn't hide her need to be near him at all times. When Jessica Knowles gave them a curious look a few days ago, she quickly put her arm around him and gave her a don't-even-think-about-it-he's-mine look.

"If there aren't any questions, we'll see everyone later at the Waterdale." Peter checked his watch. "I've got some work to do." He stood and walked away.

Church took Conner's hand. "Let's go."

———

AS THEY WALKED AWAY, BURGESS SAW DONNELLY GIVE THEM A middle finger. Burgess raised his eyebrows at the gesture and turned to see if anyone else saw the insult. He was surprised to see Jessica Knowles nod her approval. *What a dysfunctional group.*

Brenda Thompson quietly commented, "That was hardly appropriate. Even if this is a bar, shouldn't these people act like adults?"

Burgess added, "There is a difference between adults and maturity." He watched as Donnelly and Knowles left. They didn't leave together, although Donnelly took fast steps to catch up with her, trying to engage her in conversation.

Thompson nursed her gin and tonic. "Other than Tanya and Paul, the rest of the cast doesn't seem to really like each other." She smiled. "Present company excluded, of course."

He tapped his glass against hers. "Another round?"

———

"WANT TO GET A DRINK?"

Knowles inwardly sighed. She had hoped her quick pace would indicate to Donnelly that she wasn't interested in any social activity.

Certainly not with you. How you managed to get Tanya to go out with you is a mystery to me. But a bike-riding, foul-mouth man like you is of no interest to me. "Sorry, I have other plans."

"Too bad. I know of a couple of spots that you'd find interesting." Donnelly gave his best impression of being nonchalant about being turned down. "Your loss."

As if spending more time with you wouldn't be a loss. "Mitch, we play opposite each other in the play. I think it's best we keep our relationship as actors until at least the play is over. There are enough problems with the cast having relations without us adding to it."

Donnelly grunted. "See you later." He turned away and disappeared down the street.

13

STONE ROTATED A PEN BETWEEN HIS FINGERS AS HE SAT AT HIS desk. "Anya, who do you want to interview next? I don't think Carlton's parents know much about his life or have any information that could help us find his killer."

"His friends that he was hanging out with that night weren't much help either."

"So, just who would want to kill him? A drug deal gone bad? Did he owe someone money he couldn't repay?"

"He still had his wallet with money inside," Roberts pointed out.

"There is that. So maybe not about money. Revenge on something he did?"

"That's a good possibility. So, who could he have pissed off enough to kill him?"

"There was that car accident where he managed to avoid jail on a technicality. Maybe someone in the victim's family sought him out." His mobile rang, and he glanced at the number before answering it.

"Hi, Roberta. What's up?" He listened to her and, shortly later, disconnected the call.

"Was she asking you out for a coffee date?"

"No, it seems there was another development in the murder in Stony

Plain. Before Travis Moore was whacked on the head, he was hit with pepper spray. Whoever attacked him used the pepper spray first to disable him and then strike him on the head."

"That would explain just one defensive wound on one hand. He couldn't see to defend himself."

"Nasty." Stone frowned.

"Someone didn't like him very much to kill him that way. Why not just shoot him?"

"Some people always have to do things the hard way."

"Anything else they discovered?"

"No, maybe. They checked the neighbourhood for unusual vehicles parked at the time of the murder. There might have been a black pickup truck parked on a side street, also a red motorbike."

"Both of those are pretty common."

"True. Except for that red bike, I saw one on the highway when heading out to Alberta Beach on the day Moore was killed."

"Lots of red bikes."

"Yeah, I know." Stone stood. "Let's go and check on Carlton's impaired driving charge that he managed to get out of."

"Sounds like a plan."

"Actually, you check out the police records on the impaired driving charge. I'm going to get a cup of coffee."

"What a surprise."

When Stone returned carrying his cup of coffee, Roberts read out to him the information on the traffic accident. "Jacob Carlton was charged with failing to yield to a pedestrian using a crosswalk while under the influence of alcohol. According to the court documents, he blew point one four, obviously well over the impairment level. The collision occurred at five forty-seven in the evening. The victim, a Jillian Cramer, suffered permanent injuries, including losing the ability to use her legs."

"And he managed to beat the charges?"

"The police apparently didn't read him his rights properly when he was charged, so he escaped the drunk driving charges. He did plead guilty to a reduced charge of driving without due care and attention. Mitigating circumstances included the sun being in his eyes, and that she didn't stop to look for traffic before stepping out onto the road. That sounds like hogwash, but it did manage to help him avoid jail time."

"So he gets away with putting her in a wheelchair, likely with just a fine that his parents paid. Maybe she is angry enough to hire someone to have him knocked off."

"Well, that's a bit far-fetched, but it wouldn't hurt to talk to her." She passed over a piece of paper with a phone number on it.

"What's this?"

"The phone number to Jacob's brother who lives in Vancouver, Christopher Carlton. Give him a call while I get myself a tea." She gave him a smug smile and walked away.

He tapped his pen on his desk as he watched her walk away.

When Roberts returned, he informed her he had learned a few things.

"Really? What are they?"

"His brother was upset Jacob was dead and that he didn't have a clue about who did it or why. I also learned you're getting very sneaky in getting me to do work I don't like doing."

She laughed. "It's for your own good."

———

JILLIAN CRAMER LIVED IN A BUNGALOW IN THE NORTHWEST PART OF the city. The older home looked well cared for, with a wood ramp leading to the front door from the side. Roberts and Stone used the concrete steps to reach the entrance. After pushing the doorbell, they waited until the inner wood door opened, revealing a slim woman in a wheelchair, perhaps in her late thirties.

She looked puzzled at their introduction, merely glancing at their identification cards.

"How can I help you? What is this about?"

"This is about Jacob Carlton, the man who struck you in a crosswalk two years ago."

"Perhaps you should come inside."

Stone looked around the living room before sitting down on a patterned couch. The furniture was of an older style than he expected. A cross in a frame hung in the middle of a wall. The rest of the walls were devoid of decoration, save for a print of ducks in flight. He did note that the furnishings were well spaced to allow for easy movement of the wheelchair.

"May I offer you tea or coffee?"

Stone readily accepted the offer for coffee, and Roberts agreed to one as well. After Cramer left for the kitchen, Roberts asked, "Another cup of coffee? You alone might be responsible for some of the coffee plantations."

"I've discovered drinking whiskey is frowned upon when at work, so I have a java instead."

"Commendable." She looked at the ceiling.

Cramer returned with a tray on her lap.

"So, what is this about? The accident happened almost two years ago, and I settled with the insurance company five months ago. I didn't expect to hear from the police again about him."

Roberts spoke, "Jacob Carlton has been murdered."

Cramer gasped and put her hands to her face. "My God, that's awful."

"You're upset about the death of a man who caused your injuries?"

"Of course. I had to forgive him before I could appreciate what I do have. His death doesn't give me any pleasure."

"It's good that you have forgiven him. However, we are searching for clues that may have led to his death. Were you, or anyone you know, in contact with him after the accident?"

"No, other than through our lawyers."

"That must have been very difficult for you at the time."

"It was, but the Lord gave me strength. I also had the support of my family and friends. The lawyers and one of the newspaper reporters were also very understanding. They were very patient when talking to me. I met some very nice people because of the accident."

Roberts and Stone thanked her for her time and sat in Stone's Veloster.

"Nice lady, but she makes terrible coffee."

Roberts agreed and added, "She was very forgiving to Carlton for what he did."

"Yeah, she acted sincere about being upset by his death."

"What's next? Check more names on his cell phone?"

"I think so. We haven't managed to get any suspects so far. Let's hope the killer had called him at some point."

Roberts looked at the list of phone contacts in the file folder. "Okay, there's a Cory Hamilton, and we have an address."

"Okay. He's not related to you, I hope."

"No. And don't be a smart-ass."

CORY HAMILTON LIVED IN A SPRAWLING HOME, LOCATED IN THE Millwoods community. Stone drove to the residence in the deep southeast part of the city, stopping along the curb. The long driveway went past the side of the home to a three-car garage. A pair of bikes were parked in the wide driveway.

Roberts eyed the landscaped front yard.

"Well, it seems he's not hurting for money."

"A successful businessman."

"Yeah, just maybe not legally made income."

The front entrance consisted of a pair of oak doors. Stone pushed the doorbell and waited, suspecting there was a video camera observing them. Almost a minute passed before a large man opened the door halfway.

"Yeah?"

Stone looked up at the bald, bearded man. Tattoos covered his arms. His T-shirt strained against his muscles. "Police investigation. Are you Cory Hamilton?"

"No. What do you want to see him about?"

"Just information. Is he home?"

"Maybe. I'll check." He closed the door.

Stone turned to Roberts. "It seems Mr. Hamilton may or may not exist in his home until the doorman checks. A rather strange version of Schrödinger's cat."

She laughed. "You mean where the cat is simultaneously both dead and alive until someone checks to see if a vial of poison has killed it or not."

"Hey, you know quantum mechanics."

"No, I've just heard you yap about it enough times. It still doesn't make any sense to me."

The door opened again, and this time the big man signalled for them to enter. They followed him to the living room where a well-dressed man sat in an armchair.

"I'm Cory Hamilton. What can I do to help you?"

Stone was aware of the muscled tattoo man standing behind him. "We're investigating the death of Jacob Carlton. We're curious about your connection with him."

Hamilton shrugged. "Not much. We did some business dealings. Nothing big."

"Was he one of your suppliers or did he buy from you?"

A smile crossed Hamilton's face. "He bought from us. I suspect you know that already."

Stone peered at him. "Any reason why someone may want to see him dead?"

"None that I know of. He won't be missed, but as far as I know, he hadn't ruffled anyone's feathers. Like I said, minor business dealings. Sorry I can't help you." He stood.

"He didn't owe you any money?"

"No, he wouldn't get any merchandise without paying up-front. He was strictly small-time."

"Okay. Did he sound worried the last time he talked to you?"

Hamilton shook his head. "I didn't talk to him. I have an assistant to answer my business lines."

Stone and Roberts exited the house.

"That wasn't too useful," Roberts commented.

"No, other than according to Hamilton, Carlton wasn't worth much to him. He could have ordered a hit on Carlton. However, it sounds like Carlton wasn't causing any trouble."

"I guess this leaves us spinning our wheels in the investigation. Not much useful information here."

Stone continued to walk toward his car. He looked back at the house, eyeing the two big black bikes. "I wouldn't say that. Sometimes the elimination of a suspect helps to narrow our focus."

"I guess so, even though we didn't get much information here."

"I think you're forgetting that Carlton and Hamilton were connected via the drugs. That may not be the only connection."

"What do you mean?"

"I'll tell you later. My theory is still a bit sketchy."

"You and sketchy work well together."

14

TANYA CONNER REACHED THE SIDE ENTRANCE TO THE WALTERDALE Theatre. She had read up on the history of the Walterdale Theatre, finding out it was housed in a former fire hall, built in 1909. She learned that the building was apparently haunted and considered the murder of the leading man and his subsequent reappearance as a ghost in the play might be amusing to the spirit residing in the old brick building.

She saw Paul Church talking to Peter McNab or, rather, receiving a lecture from the arrogant director. She couldn't make out exactly what McNab was saying, but concluded from his rapid arm movements he was trying to convey something he considered important. The stage had three levels, each a step up from the next. The theatre style of seating curved around the front of the stage, giving performances a more intimate feel with the audience. The low ceiling and smaller space allowed for voices to be easily heard in the 150-seat venue.

Conner went to the common dressing room on the second floor, climbing the short set of narrow stairs. She entered the women's washroom and quickly changed to the outfit she was to wear on stage. One aspect of her character was a fashion designer, so she put on a skirt and patterned stockings, the kind that stayed up by themselves. Her top was a more specialized item. The form-fitting blouse had fake buttons on the outside but used Velcro to secure the front halves together. Her bra underneath was lacy but wasn't revealing. In the play, Church was to rip open her blouse, and though they had practiced the part and performed the scene in front of an audience, it still made her anxious each time it happened. Part of her emotions, she knew, were her feelings about him. In her mind, she was seriously considering that he may be the one for her.

She returned to the common dressing room where chairs were set in front of mirrors to assist in adding makeup, and went to a table where water bottles were kept in a large plastic bowl filled with ice. She opened a bottle, taking several small sips. Conner acknowledged Jessica Knowles was doing a good job as an actress and a stage manager. She did a lot of small things, such as providing for bottled water and making sure the stage was swept clean before each performance. What Conner had trouble with was Knowles switching between flirting with Church one time, and giving him and herself dirty looks minutes later. *That woman has a personality disorder.*

"So this is what it's like before the big performance."

Conner turned, and saw Janet Gourneau grinning at her. "Hey, how did you manage to get in here before the doors opened?"

"I just acted like I belonged here and no one questioned me." She hugged Conner, whispering in her ear, "You look gorgeous. This acting does something for you."

"Thanks." Conner felt a blush coming on. "I have to dress up as a bit of a tart for the role."

"No, I don't see you as a tart. Just kind of sexy." She leaned forward and gave her a brief kiss on the lips. "Sorry, I didn't mean to embarrass you."

"That's all right, I took it as a compliment."

"How about drinks after the show? I'd like to treat you for getting me the ticket."

"I'll have to check with Paul. Sometimes he has made plans but maybe the three of us can get together."

"Sure. I'll get out of your way now." She walked to where the stairs that led down to the stage and seating, frowning slightly.

Conner finished with her makeup and went downstairs to the stage and saw Church had finished with his conversation with McNab and made her way to where he sat on the stage. "What was that all about with Peter?"

"He wants more passion from me in Jaret's role." Church shrugged. "I told him I didn't think the character was meant to be the excitable kind, more like that he gets a woman by playing it cool."

"What did he say to that?"

"That he wrote the damn play and that he knows what my character is supposed to be like. He said if I didn't express more emotion, he would find someone who would."

"Jesus. Was he serious? He can't just replace the leading man. Besides, I think you're doing a great job acting." She moved closer to him. "I do look forward to our kissing scenes."

He smiled. "Thanks, so do I. Janet has arrived early, I see."

"Yeah. She wants to have drinks with us after the show."

"Sure. I'll likely be able to use a drink by then."

———

CHURCH DID AS THE SCRIPT DIRECTED, WALKING TO THE BACK OF the set to where Conner, who played the role of Veronica, talked to Donnelly. Church refilled his plastic tumbler, meant to look like a whiskey glass, with iced tea. It was the only tumbler used in the play, the rest being wineglasses and beer cans.

He tried to show more emotion, as McNab wanted, when he returned to where Conner and Donnelly stood. He looked forward to the next scene where he would follow the character Veronica to the kitchen. There, he didn't have to worry about showing any emotions. He felt a surge of excitement at the thought of kissing Conner and pulling open her shirt.

Conner followed her lines, complaining to Church that he forgot her wine.

"Where's my wine? Did you drink it carrying it over here?" Conner laughed at her joke.

"The bottle was empty. What else would you like to have?" Church passed over a can of beer to Donnelly.

"I believe there is more wine in the kitchen. I'll take a look." She gave

Church a smile and walked across the stage where the kitchen part of the stage was set up.

Church leered at Conner as she made her way to the kitchen. "I should go and help her look."

Church walked across the stage to the kitchen, now dark as Donnelly and the others acted out their parts in the living room part of the stage. He whispered hello to Conner and then remained quiet. He felt Conner's hand search out his, and he closed his fingers around hers. They waited in dark shadows, observing part of the living room stage and the audience, and listened to the rehearsed lines of the actors.

Minutes passed and the lights came on in the kitchen.

Conner followed the script, obtaining a bottle of wine from the cabinet. "See, I know where the wine is kept."

"A smart girl like you likely knows a lot of things."

Church moved closer to her and put his arm around her waist. He leaned forward, preparing to kiss Conner.

Conner grinned. "Now, I have to ask, are you going to start something you can't finish? Because it seems to me that you just might be the teasing type." Conner kissed him, placing the bottle of wine on the counter and wrapping her arms around his neck to kiss him again. She leaned back, giving Church the opportunity to kiss her neck.

Church felt her hands slide down his arms as she leaned back, the cue for him to pull open her top.

"Oh! You're such a bad boy."

"But you like it." He pushed her toward the kitchen table and placed his hands on her waist, lifting her on top of it. He began to climb on the table as well and then the studio lights in the kitchen set of the play went off.

Conner whispered in the dark, "I do like our kissing scenes."

"I prefer kissing you when we're alone but this will do as well." His hand slid up her rib cage.

"That feels nice but let's not go too far here." Her hand pressed against his arm.

"It's dark, no one can see us."

"Wanna bet that someone can't make out what we're doing?"

"All right." He kissed her, pressing against her as they listened to the voices coming from the living room set.

"Hey, that's our cue." Conner heard the line from the living room, signifying for them to turn the table on its side. She helped Church turn the table on its side and then allowed it to drop a short distance to the floor. The kitchen floodlights came back on as the other actors arrived in the kitchen.

———

CONNER THOUGHT THE PLAY WENT WELL, THE AUDIENCE LAUGHED at the appropriate moments and no one forgot or mispoke their lines. She did understand what McNab said about Church; he wasn't used to performing in front of a crowd, and his style of acting was stiff and without a lot of facial expressions. *But this is his first acting experience. Peter shouldn't have put so much pressure on a new actor, who is supposed to be cool and confident. Paul does do better in his second role as Detective Harry Rush where he gets to act a bit clumsy.*

Conner was referring to where Church's first character, Jaret, was murdered and then returned as Detective Harry Rush. She thought McNab had been clever in using the same actor for two roles to add a comedic touch, but that's where her admiration for the playwright ended.

The play was nearly finished. Conner was close by where Church was upstairs in the common dressing room. Jessica Knowles applied a dusting of white powder to Church's face and neck. He was to make a final appearance as a ghost to end the play and the white powder was to give the illusion he was a spirit. She overheard Knowles speak as she finished with the white dust.

"There. *Now* you're a dead man."

Conner didn't hear any humour in the statement and was getting tired of her obvious dislike for Church and herself. *I'll be glad when the play is done and we don't have to work with her anymore.*

———

SHE RETURNED DOWNSTAIRS AND, ALONG WITH THE REST OF THE

cast, watched and listened as Church made a final speech standing in the kitchen, holding a wineglass.

"Don't be alarmed. I'm quite dead and not the zombie kind of dead either. I'm just a ghost. A ghost that can drink wine may seem unusual, but I assure you there are stranger things in this world than that." He walked from the kitchen to the centre of the stage.

"It has been said, all the world is a stage, and men and women are merely players. If that is true, then the players on this stage wish to thank this audience for coming to our play and we hope you enjoyed *Death of a Philanderer.*"

Conner walked onto the stage behind Church, and the rest of the cast followed her. They formed a line behind Church and joined hands. The audience applauded, they bowed twice and exited the stage.

Church returned upstairs. He wiped the powder from his face and neck with a cloth in front of the table and mirrors. He used the men's washroom to change his shirt. The dressing room had several mirrors in front of a long table. Comfortable chairs were placed at intervals to allow for applying makeup. The rest of the room held a round table with plastic and metal chairs surrounding it. The ladies' and men's washrooms were featured along one wall, each with a notice not to flush the toilet during performances. He called out to the door to the women's washroom.

"I'll see you downstairs."

"Okay, I won't be long."

Church went downstairs and exited down a short hallway, spotting Burgess standing near the entrance to the building.

"That went pretty good. The audience gave us a lot of applause at the end." Burgess then gave Church a compliment. "You did a good job on your scenes, Peter's criticism notwithstanding."

"Thanks, I appreciate that." Conner looked down the hallway where they were standing and saw Janet Gourneau waiting by the theatre's entrance. "Excuse me, I better see what she is up to."

"Hi, Janet."

"Hey there." She gave him a half smile. "Are you joining us for drinks?"

He frowned, "Yeah, I will be. Tanya and I usually go for drinks after performances and practice. But it will be nice to have you as company as well."

Conner came down the stairs. She looked between Gourneau and Church, noticing a bit of tension between them. "Are we ready for drinks?"

Gourneau and Church readily agreed and they made their way from the theatre to Old Town Pub on Whyte Avenue. They sat in the patio area, enjoying the outside air after the time spent inside during the play. The waitress greeted them, then asked, "I need to see your ID. Liquor inspectors are making the rounds here."

Conner understood the reason for the request. Anyone who looked twenty-five years of age or younger had to be checked. If they weren't, the bar could receive large fines. She passed over her driver's licence. The server checked it and next took Gourneau's produced identification. She gave a smile and returned the laminated card.

Church was on the opposite side of the table from the waitress and had to stretch out his arm to pass over his driver's licence. After it was inspected, the waitress extended her hand toward him. Conner took the card from her and began to pass it to Church. She glanced at the card and inspected it closer.

"Hey, Paul is your second name."

Church nodded. "Yeah, I like Paul better than Terrence."

"Both are nice."

Janet peered at the driver's licence as it went by her but didn't voice a comment.

Conversation changed, and as drinks were consumed, Conner pressed Gourneau on what she thought of the play. "Truthfully. What can we do better? Did you really enjoy the play?"

"Well, I thought it was a good murder mystery of the lighthearted kind. There were some funny lines, and overall, I enjoyed the play. It was geared for adults, with your top being ripped open. I actually enjoyed that bit the most."

"And the acting?"

"I'm not much of a live theatre goer myself, so it's hard to judge. But maybe some of the lack of acting experience did come through. I still enjoyed it and would recommend it to others."

Church changed the subject, believing Gourneau was hinting about his lack of practise as an actor. "What do you do for a living, Janet?"

She brushed her finger through her hair and gave a grin. "I'm a bit of a free spirit."

Conner laughed, "No kidding."

Gourneau continued after giggling. "I'm actually a journalist but pick my spots on what to write about. I went to New Zealand and worked as a waitress while I wrote a travel book on the South Island. Before then, I lived here in Edmonton and wrote a bunch of human-interest stories for *The Edmonton Journal*. That was okay but I got a rather jaded view of humanity while doing some of the stories."

"In what way?"

"Let's just say some people screw up other people's lives and they don't learn they shouldn't do what they did again. I guess I'm tired of seeing the same problems keep repeating."

"Some people do learn from mistakes. No one is perfect." Church peered at her and slowly lifted his beer to his mouth.

———

"Would you like a ride home?" Church directed his question to Gourneau at the end of the evening.

"Thanks, but I have my own wheels." She gave Conner a kiss on her cheek and whispered, "I'll call you tomorrow."

Church walked hand in hand with Conner to his car, an older Toyota Camry. "Janet seems okay, although a little strange."

"That sums her up all right. But she really does have a passionate side that, that... makes her special."

Church started the Camry. "Can we talk? There's something I want to tell you."

"Sure. Let's go to my place." She watched the buildings flow past as the car headed north. "What do you want to talk about? Janet? Us?"

"No, something about me you should know. I don't want to tell you while I'm driving."

"Okay." Conner looked at Church, his eyes focused on the road ahead of him. She noticed that when he drove, his full attention went on driving and conversation was sparse. They crossed the North Saskatchewan River, following the curved road that climbed the river bank.

He broke the silence. "Janet said something about people not learning from their mistakes. I made a big mistake a while back. Something awful. I need to tell you about it, so you know who I am and if you want to continue to go out with me."

"Okay, but I think I already know you."

"Maybe you do. But you need to know the truth why I moved from Calgary."

He parked the Camry and they walked up the stairs to her apartment. Conner pulled out a bottle of Tennessee Whiskey, poured two glasses and added ice cubes. She handed one glass to Church. "Okay, let's talk. What happened in Calgary?"

Church slouched on the couch, took a drink, and closed his eyes. "I killed a girl."

Conner gasped, her eyes wide as she stared at him. She shared the couch with him, sitting sideways with one leg curled under her.

He looked across the room, seeing the past. "It was a Saturday afternoon. I had a couple of beers with a buddy at his place to watch a game. It was a soccer game. Doesn't matter. On the way home I remember changing the radio station. I looked down for just a second. Then, she was there, running across the middle of a street." His jaw tightened, and his voice stalled.

Conner placed a hand on his arm, waiting for him to continue. Seconds passed.

"I hardly had time to hit the brakes." He shook his head slowly and finished off the whiskey. "She died right there. The cops tried to charge me with impaired, but there was no way two drinks put me over the limit. The judge dismissed all charges but all I can remember is the sound of her hitting the hood of my car."

"It doesn't sound like it was your fault. She ran onto the street. You couldn't stop."

"Maybe. But I did glance down at the damn radio. I'll never get rid of that moment as long as I live."

"I understand."

"That's why I started using Paul as my first name and why I moved to Edmonton. I needed to start fresh, to leave what happened in Calgary behind. It was either that or go crazy."

Conner stood and went to the kitchen, bringing back the bottle of whiskey. She added the gold liquid to his glass, noting the ice still hadn't had a chance to dissolve yet.

"Thanks. Now that you know, do you still want to go out with me?"

Conner put her glass on the coffee table. She sat on his lap, kissing him on the lips. "I don't have to answer that, do I?" She kissed him again. "I know who you are."

15

Moss Stone dropped into his office chair, clutching a coffee cup. He looked over at his partner and offered a tired, "Good morning."

"It's morning, all right." She clicked a few keys on her keyboard and studied the monitor for a moment. "What do we do about our Carlton investigation? So far, we haven't had much luck with our interviews or any other leads." She clicked another key on her keyboard. "His car didn't show anything unexpected. Fast food wrappers, a package of cigarettes, an empty pop can, a small amount of pot in the glove compartment, and a half tank of gas."

"I guess we recycle. We redo the interviews and dig out more information. Maybe we can find something else in his past." He pondered his coffee momentarily. "Was there anything unusual in his wallet?"

"No, a couple of twenties and three fives. His driver's licence, a library card, of all things, and a credit card. Not much else."

"Let's see where he's used the credit card. Maybe where he used it will tell us something."

"Okay, I'll get a list."

THE CREDIT CARD PURCHASE LIST DIDN'T REVEAL ANYTHING unusual. The use of the card revealed when he may have been short of cash. Purchases were bunched together and then stopped. A week or two later the card use increased again.

Stone and Roberts did stop at the Domo gas station and the convenience stores, but the clerks didn't recall anything about his visits. The liquor store, Kegs and More, did offer slightly more information.

Moss and Roberts entered what appeared to be a small store in the west end of the city. A sign on the wood door pleaded to keep the door closed as, "The dog is an escape artist." Slightly amused at the handwritten sign, Moss scanned the basic shelves holding various alcoholic products. A few cases of wine were stacked on the floor, with another sign showing the reduced price.

"Can I help you?" a voice growled at him.

Stone turned to the man sitting behind the counter. He was a big man and his face didn't reveal whether he was friendly or not.

Roberts spoke up, showing her police identification. "We're investigating the murder of Jacob Carlton. It seems he made a few purchases here."

"Jacob Carlton? Skinny dude?" He paused, "I'm Mark, by the way."

Stone stepped forward. "Yeah, that'd be him. Know anything about him?"

"Not much. He came in here a few times. Sometimes paid cash, other times a credit card. He'd chat us up and then ask for a better deal on beer. I felt a bit sorry for him, he looked poor, and I'd try to save him a bit of dough."

"You do that a lot, bargain prices?"

"No, just in certain cases. Good karma to help out others."

Stone nodded, starting to like the man behind the counter. "This seems like an odd location for a liquor store. It can't be that busy here."

"You should see the back. The rest of the store is mostly warehouse. A bulk of our business is to licensees. We supply a lot of bars. The liquor store part is just a convenience for our customers."

"Interesting. Getting back to Carlton, do you know of anyone who would want to do him harm? Did he ever come in with anyone?"

Mark shook his head. "No on both counts. Sorry, all we did was sell him beer."

Stone picked up a bottle of wine. "Good price for a California pinot noir."

"Yeah, we have a lower markup. Buy a whole case and I'll give you an even better deal."

"I'll keep that in mind. Thanks for your help."

"No problem."

Roberts walked back with Stone to his car. "What do you think?"

"I think this may be a good place to buy booze."

"I mean about Carlton."

"I think Carlton knew where he could get a fair price on beer. Other than that, nothing."

"Then I guess it's back to interviewing."

"It is. Let's go to his parents first."

———

JOSEPH AND MARLENE CARLTON WERE PLEASANT WHEN THE detectives appeared at their home again.

Joseph Carlton immediately asked, "Can you tell us of the progress you've made in finding Jacob's killer? Do you have any suspects?"

Stone replied, "We're currently reviewing information, although we don't have a suspect yet. You mentioned before that Jacob was involved in a car accident that left the victim partially paralyzed. Do you recall any more details regarding the settlement?"

"There isn't much more to tell. It was basically handled by the insurance company. I believe Jacob had to appear in court and explain the events of that night."

"Was there any contact between Jacob and the victim afterward? Or even from her family or friends?"

"Not that I'm aware of. Of course, Jacob didn't keep in touch with us, so I guess we wouldn't know if someone from her family contacted him."

"Who was his lawyer?"

Carlton walked to the dining room and opened a drawer of a small corner table. He returned with a business card. "Here's the law office that we used."

Marlene asked, "Do you think someone from her family had something to do with Jacob's death?"

"We're just following up all possible leads. At the present time, we don't have any reason to believe Jillian Cramer or her family are responsible for what happened to Jacob."

"Then why do you want to see the lawyer we used?"

Stone put the business card in his shirt pocket. "Because everything is connected."

———

Roberts closed the passenger door of the Veloster. "What's this about the 'everything is connected' answer you gave to Marlene Carlton?"

He passed over the business card of the lawyer. "Look at the names on the card."

"Benson, Kirkman, Ines, and Edwards. Attorneys at law. So?"

"The first letter of each name. If you swap the middle names, you get the word bike. One of the neighbours where Carlton was killed heard a bike go by the evening he was killed."

"What? How does that mean anything?" She stared at him. "Isn't that a little far-fetched, even for you?"

"I say we go and visit the lawyer, or do you have a better suggestion?"

"We should stop by a drugstore first and see if they have reality pills you can take."

"You may laugh, but everywhere we go searching for Carlton's killer, something about bikes appear. I promise you that when we find his killer there will be a bike in the equation."

Roberts remained silent, remembering how often he solved cases with his strange logic.

———

THE OFFICE WAS LOCATED IN THE MANULIFE TOWER, INDICATING

they were successful and not overly concerned about their clients' difficulty to find parking. The elevator took them quickly to the floor entirely occupied by the law firm. The receptionist at the law firm stared at them with a blank expression when Roberts informed her they wanted to talk to the lawyer who looked after the Jacob Carlton accident.

"I think that was a long time ago. I'll have to check our files. May I ask what this is concerning?"

Stone looked around the large reception area with comfortable-looking furniture, leaving Roberts to convince the receptionist of the requirement to divulge the name of the particular lawyer.

"Jacob Carlton was murdered. We're looking for possible motives."

"Oh." The woman suddenly took an interest in their request and began the arduous task of accessing files on her computer. "That would be Dianna Ines." She pressed a button on her phone. "Dianna, are you free to talk to the police about one of your former clients?" A moment later, she spoke to the detectives. "She'll be just a few minutes. Can I get you water or a coffee?"

Stone quickly replied. "I take my coffee black."

———

Ten minutes later, a smiling Dianna Ines greeted them. "I'm sorry to have kept you waiting." She escorted them to her office, which offered a window view of the various cranes used to lift buildings from holes in the ground.

Stone explained about the murder of Jacob Carlton and that they were looking for anyone that may have held a grudge against him.

Ines looked inside a yellow file folder, flipping through pages. "I recall the case. You said Jacob Carlton was murdered?"

"Yes, gunshot in a school parking lot."

Ines nodded. "I read in the paper of a murder in the west end. It feels different when you can place a face to it." She looked at them. "I don't know what I can tell you that may be of help. Our firm defended him in court, and we had some dealings with the insurance company and Jillian Cramer, the victim in the accident. Jillian Cramer didn't sound hostile when I talked with her briefly. Obviously, most of my dealings were with her lawyer. It wasn't an emotional settlement, where the victim was listing a lot of issues besides the physical injuries. I'm sorry, I can't be more of help to you."

"What was your impression of Jacob?"

Ines paused before she spoke. "He came from a loving, religious family, so he had a better upbringing than most. But he seemed to resent the help his parents were providing and didn't show any remorse for the suffering he caused Jillian Cramer. He was a self-centered man."

"I see. What was the name of Jillian Cramer's lawyer?"

"Henry Stevenson. His office is in Scotia Place."

"Another downtown office building." He sighed.

Ines smiled. "Lawyers do tend to congregate downtown. Sorry."

"That's all right. We'll give them a visit tomorrow."

16

PETER McNAB READ THE LATEST REVIEWS AND REMARKS ABOUT HIS play. He hated having to use his computer this much, constantly refreshing the screen to see any new comments about *Death of a Philanderer*. Generally, the play received positive notes. The ratings ranged from three to four stars out of five. That meant it was well liked but fell well short of his expectations. The casual theatregoer was generally more favourable in their assessment but the local newspapers were harsh in their appraisal. He read out loud the review by Kerry Jones, a well-known columnist who covered the arts in a weekly newspaper feature.

"*Death of a Philanderer* has some interesting moments but *just* fails to reach the level it is capable of. Obviously, the play is meant to be a dark comedy, but the wooden acting undermines its success. Some of the lines were delivered so flat, the audience was left wondering if they should laugh or remain silent. The play opens where a house party was taking place, and one should assume the characters were all familiar with each other. Instead, the acting led us to believe they were merely strangers placed together. I give this play three popcorn kernels. Perhaps by the end of the Fringe festival our actors will be more comfortable performing in front of an audience."

He slapped his hand on the desk, crossed his arms, and glared at the offending screen. Words taunted him as he read other reviews.

"Good play, but in the end, not memorable."

"The play showed promise, but I can't say it delivered. Just sort of petered out."

"*Death of a Philanderer* came so close, but next week no one will remember it."

His teeth worked against themselves. His arms moved about, crossed again, and finally cradled his neck.

"Damn actors. It's a great play. If only they could act out their lines and characters the way I intended." He stood. "I gave Paul the lead role. Why the hell couldn't he focus on the play as much as he does on that damn woman?" He paced about the tiny room available in his office, his voice gaining substance. "It's his fault my play—my play!—is not receiving the recognition it deserves. He shall pay the price for this fiasco." He breathed in slowly, and in his best Shakespearean voice bellowed, "Boldness be my friend!"

———

CONNER OPENED HER APARTMENT DOOR. "HI, JANET."

"Hi, Tanya." Gourneau stepped inside the living room. "I brought wine." She smiled as she held the bottle in the air.

"I'll get the glasses." Conner went to the kitchen. "What did you want to see me about? It sounded important in your text."

"A couple of things." She poured wine into the two glasses and took one from Conner. "I see we're alone."

"Paul had some things to do. He'll be back later to drive me for the next performance."

"Okay." She held up her glass. "To us."

Conner touched her glass against Gourneau's. "To us." She sat on the couch, joining Gourneau, and took a drink of her wine. "You wanted to talk, so, here we are."

"What do you know about Paul?"

"A fair bit. Why?"

"Do you know what happened in Calgary with Paul? He ran over a little girl after drinking." Gourneau watched Conner's face after her revelation.

"I know, he told me. He wasn't drunk. That little girl ran right in front of him. There wasn't anything he could do."

"Maybe. It looks like he didn't have to pay for her death. No fine or time in jail. Hell, he didn't even have his licence suspended."

Conner crossed her arms. "How do you know this?"

"I'm a reporter. I know how to dig up facts."

"Okay, the *fact* is he was so distraught about what happened, he started using his second name and moved here. He paid plenty for what happened in Calgary. Not in money or in jail time, but in his mind. He's a good man, and a terrible thing happened, but that doesn't change that he's a good man."

Gourneau was silent, thinking. "Okay, maybe I was wrong. It sounds like he's okay after all. I didn't want to see you get hurt by a guy that wasn't being honest with you."

"He's honest with me. I trust him."

"All right." She took another drink of her wine and refilled the glass. "I'm going back to New Zealand at the end of the month. Tanya, I never stopped loving you. I know this sounds sudden but will you think about joining me in New Zealand? You can stay as long as you want. No pressure. I realize I miss you so much."

Conner dropped her jaw slightly. "I can't, as much as I care for you too, I just can't. My life is here. And there's Paul. I feel very close to him. I think he's a perfect man for me. Jan, what we had was wonderful and you'll always be more than just a friend to me." She took her hand. "We'll always be connected, even when you live half a world away."

"Thanks. I had to ask."

"More wine?"

———

PAUL WAS SURPRISED WHEN HE RETURNED TO CONNER'S apartment. The two women were sitting close to each other on the couch and giggling over a private joke. Gourneau noticed him, stood, and finished off the bit of wine in her glass.

"I best be going." She walked up to Church and placed a hand on his shoulder as she walked past him. "Take good care of her. She's very special."

"You don't have to tell me that."

———

After Gourneau left, Church poured himself a drink. "Did you have a good time with Janet?" He looked at the glasses on the table.

"We did. We talked about the old times we had together. But that's in the past. This is the present and I'm here with you."

He smiled. "All right. It's good you connected with her again."

"Thanks. Can you drive me in the morning to the Walterdale? I know parking is a hassle but the bus to get there takes forever."

"Not a problem."

———

In the morning, Paul Church dropped Conner off near the Walterdale Theatre and then drove to park a few blocks away. The popularity of the Fringe had swallowed much of the parking, forcing a desperate search for spots that evaporated faster than a cold beer on a hot day. He finally found a parking spot and made his way to the theatre, drinking from a bottle of water. He made his way to the stage, he saw that Peter McNab was acting even more agitated than usual. He went to the back of the stage area and exchanged a kiss with Tanya Conner.

"What's with Peter?"

Conner pulled his arm, leading him away from others nearby. She whispered to him. "It's not good. He muttered that tonight could be the last performance for some of us. He ranted something about all of us needing acting lessons and he mentioned your name in particular."

"Shit."

"I don't know if it means anything, but I saw Dana Sharpe here earlier. She came in through the actors' door as if she belonged to our troupe and then just walked around saying hello to everyone."

"Did she say why she was here?"

"She mumbled something about wanting to see the play she almost had a part in."

"Where is she now?"

Conner waved a hand at the dark area where the audience sat. "Somewhere out there. She went to sit where the seating is."

"Interesting and a little strange."

Tyler Burgess came up to them. "Have you noticed anything peculiar going on here?"

Church responded, "What do you mean? Besides Dana being here."

"That man standing next to Peter. He's an actor, I think his name is Crestman. In any event, I saw him last year in a play. Quite good. But I wonder what he may be conversing with our director about. A possible replacement for one of our characters, perhaps?"

Conner frowned. "If that's what Peter is planning, then he's gone too far."

Church crossed his arms. "To hell with him. Let's put on our play and make the audience love us."

"Tanya."

Conner looked over to where people were filing into the seats. "Jan! What are you doing here?"

Janet Gourneau held up a ticket. "I thought I should support you and the play by actually buying a ticket." She gave Conner a long hug, and a kiss on the cheek. She looked at Church. "Nice seeing you again, Paul." Her smile was brief.

Paul nodded. "You're getting to be a regular live theatregoer."

"I know what I like." She glanced at Conner, "I better sit down and let you guys get ready."

Conner called out as Gourneau walked away. "Perhaps we'll see you after the show."

Gourneau replied as she twisted back, "Can't. I have another commitment."

Church put his arm around Conner's waist. "I think she's a little too interested in the play or, at least, in one of the performers."

"Sorry, I know how it looks. But while I do care for her, it's you I want to be with. I promise there's no desire for me to be other than a friend to her."

"Okay, thanks." They broke apart as they reached the back of the stage. "Time to change and kick some butt on our performances."

———

CHURCH STOOD IN THE CENTRE OF THE STAGE, LISTENING TO Brenda Thompson speak. He felt too warm in his trench coat as he acted out his second character in the play, Harry Rush. So far, the audience was enjoying the play, laughing at the lines and antics of the characters. Unlike the first few performances, he felt at ease and more comfortable with his lines and that seemed to make a huge difference on how the crowd was reacting to the murder mystery. The other personnel in the play took a cue from him. They all seemed more relaxed and able to present the play as it was intended.

"I thought he was cute. We had sex a few times. And he was a very good dancer."

"I thought you went out with Jon?"

"I did. Also, with Jaret. Also, with... Let's just say I'm a people person."

The audience laughed as Thompson gave a shrug and a smile.

"This is all very interesting but one of you did murder this poor handsome fella." Harry referred to his first character, Jaret, who now was represented by cushions under a blanket. Some of the audience understood his self-compliment and chuckled.

Church began to nibble from the food platter on a coffee table. After a couple of bites, he picked up a knife to cut a slice of cheese.

Immediately, Jessica Knowles exclaimed, "What are you doing?! What if that's the knife used to stab Jaret?"

Church acted startled and began to juggle the knife before it fell to the floor. He made an exaggerated jump back as he peered at the knife. "Stabbed with this knife? Why am I the last to know how he was killed?"

Church raised his arms in the air, clearly showing his annoyance. He heard the laughter from beyond the stage, pleased at their response. "Well, this actually helps a lot."

The professor, played by Burgess, asked, "How? By touching the knife you've put your own fingerprints on it over the killer's."

Church responded by lifting his nose in the air and lectured, "Your comment is something someone less skilled in detective work would make. However, this knife was not the weapon used to commit murder." He picked up the knife, waving it around for emphasis. The rest of the actors stepped back away from him. "You see, there isn't any blood on this knife. Therefore, it was not used to kill our victim. That means the real knife used in this hideous crime is still here."

Church could only make out the rows of the seats closest to the stage. From what he could see, the audience was peering intently at him, listening to him speak. *This is how it's supposed to work.*

———

CHURCH ESCORTED BURGESS OFF THE STAGE, ARRESTING HIM FOR the murder of Church's first character, Jaret, in the play. Once out of sight of the audience, Church hurried to the dressing room upstairs to change into the clothes of Jaret. Church's final appearance was now the spirit of Jaret, thanking the spectators for attending the play, *Death of a Philanderer.* Jaret wore a long-sleeved shirt, which covered his arms, but the rest of his exposed skin needed to be white to give a white ghostly appearance. Church put on white latex gloves, and Jessica Knowles entered the dressing room.

"Great job acting." She sat next to Church in front of the long makeup table. "We have had our differences but this performance went well."

"Thanks."

"Now, let's get you into the spirit of things."

Church chuckled. "Now, that was funny."

As Jessica Knowles struggled to open the container of Kryolan white powder, Church looked up seeing Conner enter the dressing room, giving him a lover's smile. Behind her, leaning against the doorframe, Burgess stood watching.

Knowles finally twisted the lid off the powder container. "That's odd. I'm sure I didn't leave it on this tight last time." She let the lid roll on the tabletop and picked up one of the brushes lying on the table. She quickly applied the white powder on his face using a wide brush on his forehead and cheeks. Next, she used a smaller brush on the areas near his eyes and nose.

"Okay, all done." She gave a smirk. "You actually look pretty good as a ghost."

Suddenly, a squeal came from the open doorway. Church and the others looked over, and Burgess peered down the stairwell. He returned his gaze to the others in the dressing room. "Nothing serious. Brenda found a spider on her arm."

Church grinned. "I was worried for a moment Harry Rush would have another murder to solve."

The others laughed.

Church stood. "Okay, let's finish the play." He walked back downstairs and entered the stage where the kitchen was situated in the play.

The lights came on and he repeated his final lines of the play. "... It has been said, all the world is a stage, and men and women are merely players. If that is true, then the players in this stage wish to thank this audience for coming to our play, and we hope you enjoyed *Death of a Philanderer*." He raised his glass of wine to the audience and took a drink.

Suddenly, he felt dizzy. Confused, he placed the wineglass on the kitchen table and used his hand on the table edge to steady himself. He took in several slow breaths and half stumbled to the doorway leading to the living room.

With his monologue complete, the rest of the cast entered the centre of the living room stage and he joined them, standing in front of them. He gasped for his breath, trying to focus on the crowd at the edge of the stage. As the audience applauded, he bowed with the rest of the performers.

He made his way toward the exit of the stage, only partially aware of someone speaking to him.

Tanya Conner whispered to him, "You killed it. Now Peter can take it and shove it. We're now all actors who performed a play the audience loved."

He walked off stage, gripping Tanya's hand.

"After you change, let's go for a celebration drink."

"Yeah, sure."

"Are you okay?"

"Just a bit dizzy." The words rushed out.

"I'll help you to the dressing room." Conner took his arm and helped him upstairs and to the makeup table. "Do you need help changing, taking off the makeup?"

"No, I'll be fine." He waited until Conner left, and began to wipe off the white powder, tossing the tissues into the garbage along with his gloves. The dizziness faded, and he changed his shirt. He looked around the dressing room, feeling confused, and exited the room.

———

CHURCH SAW THE OTHERS HAD ALREADY GATHERED AT THE SIDE exit of the building. "Sorry, I guess I'm the slow one here."

Conner gave him a hug. "That's okay. Are you all right?"

"I don't know. I've got a headache. I don't feel so good."

"Do you want to just go home?"

Before he could reply, several of the other actors congratulated him on his performance, letting him know he played his part perfectly. The lone exception was Donnelly, who ignored him. Donnelly did interact with the others briefly in one-sentence conversations.

———

TYLER BURGESS FELT GOOD ABOUT OVERCOMING HIS OWN nervousness. He noted that McNab had again turned down the offer to join the troupe in a celebratory drink, suspecting he didn't want to lower himself to the level of mere actors. Donnelly, he decided, still was jealous of Church landing the leading role. Although a young woman was hugging his arm, Burgess could tell by his frequent glances he still had eyes for Conner. *What a bit of a soap opera there is among this group. Jessica has eyes for Paul and not always the friendly kind either. I wonder what their history is? And what is Dana Sharpe doing here, joining in this group? What is she up to? A strange group indeed, and all drawn to a play that involves a murder written by a man with an ego bigger than the play itself.*

Burgess followed his fellow actors out to the lobby, where a few of the theatre patrons recognized them. The actors, surprised at their newfound popularity, graciously conversed with whoever wanted to say hello. A couple of autographs were also handed out, with Church receiving the most attention.

Burgess wasn't asked for any autographs, although a couple of ladies told him how they liked the play and his performance in it. He smiled nervously, not adept at being the centre of attention. He did mumble his thanks and appreciation and was glad he was able to continue his journey out of the lobby and into the cooler evening air.

He increased his pace to catch up to the others when he saw Church bend over. He heard him gasp, his mouth wide open. Then, in slow motion, Church bent at the knees and tumbled to the ground. Burgess couldn't see Church easily at that point as the others crowded around him but saw his legs twitch. He reached Donnelly, who stood a few feet away with his hands in his pockets. His girlfriend, he observed, looked more concerned about Church's condition than Donnelly.

More passersby joined the circle around the prone Church. Conner wailed as she tried to shake his shoulders.

A young man pushed his way through. "I'm a nurse. What happened? Did he have an attack?" He pressed his fingers against Church's neck. "Someone call 9-1-1!" He began to apply pressure on the chest of the lifeless body.

Burgess watched without emotion. Two uniformed first aid practitioners ran to Church and immediately took over from the nurse. The nurse stood, watching, and slowly shook his head. Burgess watched the scene unravel. A police officer pushed the crowd back from close proximity, and then, they began to ask questions and jotted down names. He saw Brenda Thomson comfort Conner as she sobbed on her shoulder. Burgess didn't know what to do as he took in the overwhelming emotion.

"Sir, your name, sir?"

Burgess looked at the cop staring at him. "Sorry, Officer. Tyler

Burgess." He dug out one of his business cards, containing his contact information.

"Okay, someone will contact you later." A pause. "Are you all right?"

Burgess processed the question. "Yes, thank you. I'm okay." *A death in real life is a lot different from the fictional murders I read about. I need a good stiff drink or two.*

17

THE CRAFT BEER MARKET WAS NOISY. MUSIC AND LOUD VOICES bounced off the hard surfaces of wood and furniture, making conversation difficult. The restaurant had made its reputation on serving fifty different types of beer on tap. Even wine was served from kegs and the mostly millennial-age group had a lot of choices on the beverage menu.

Anya Roberts sipped her wheat beer, quickly taking glances at one of the servers. When her girlfriends suggested they get together for a few drinks, she readily agreed. They choose to meet at the Craft Beer Market and suddenly Anya had some apprehension.

Her detective partner, Moss Stone, had a girlfriend who worked there. She had heard his description of her well enough that she felt she could guess which one of the pretty women that waitressed was Cindy. She declined to admit she had jealous feelings for him and convinced herself that her interest was strictly because she was friends with him. *Damn. Nice hair, easy smile, and she's tall.* She felt a poke at her arm and looked over at Monique sitting next to her.

Monique smiled. "I was asking you about work and that cute detective you're working with but it seems you're really into that waitress."

Anya blushed. "No, it's just that I think I know her from somewhere."

"Then go and say hello." Jennifer laughed. "Maybe she likes you, too."

"I don't think so. You were asking about Moss?"

"Just curious. How is it working with him after you-know-what happened with him a few years back?"

Anya rolled her eyes. "Ancient history. We're just friends now." She knew her friends weren't going to let her forget she slept with Stone twice before being moved in the police department to be his detective partner. What she didn't tell Monique was he had stayed overnight at her place a few weeks ago when he had too much to drink. He did sleep on the couch but her friends would interpret that as a sign they were getting closer.

"Very good friends?"

"End of discussion. No more Moss conversation."

"All right. So how do you happen to know this waitress? She's rather pretty."

"I don't know her. She's just familiar, that's all. Can I interrogate you now about your love life?"

"Nothing to tell. I'm happily single. Men call me, buy me drinks, and give me flowers on my birthday. All is how it should be." She paused. "But you, with your heart still longing for Moss Stone, have a much more complicated love life."

No kidding. Complicated. "No, my love life is dull. No boyfriend. As for Moss, we have an understanding. Just work friends."

"You're such a liar."

After two rounds of drinks, the group decided it was time to hit another bar within walking distance. There were several bars close by, and as Anya made her way to the exit, she took another look at the server. The server smiled and walked over to her.

Oh my God, she must think I was flirting with her.

"Hi, I'm Cindy. You must be Anya."

"That's right."

"Moss has told me a lot about you, so I feel I already know you. I guess you recognized me too from what Moss said."

"Yes, sorry for staring. I wasn't sure."

"That's okay." She scribbled on a piece of paper. "Here's my number. Let's have a coffee sometime."

Roberts left the bar, catching up to the others. Her phone hummed and rang. She dug it out of her purse and recognized the number. *Shit.*

———

CHRIS ARMSTRONG LEANED OVER THE POOL TABLE, PULLING HIS cue back. He froze in position for a moment before sending the cue ball rolling down the green carpet and smartly striking the black ball into the corner pocket.

Stone put his own cue stick away, separating the two halves and placing them in the case. "Nice shot."

"Thanks." He walked back to the high table where they were sitting, finished his beer and signalled the waitress for another. "How come you're out by yourself tonight? Cindy working?"

"Yeah. That's the trouble with dating a waitress. They work too many nights."

"Doesn't she also go to university? That must make it hard to find time to hang out."

"It does. She's planning to take in the Fringe in the next few days, so she'll be busy for a while."

"I went last year. It was okay, but it's not for everyone."

"I looked at the plays and there are some strange names to the plays. Hard to tell what it's about. I'd rather just relax with a drink in a bar."

"I hear you, but you want to keep her happy, too."

"Yeah, gotta find that middle ground where she's happy and I'm not bored." Stone finished his pint. "Okay, that's it for me tonight."

Armstrong laughed. "Come on. One more game." He glanced at the pool tables.

"Army, you beat me in six out of the eight games. As much fun as it has been losing to you, I think it's best that I go home while I'm still legally allowed to do so." He stood, easing the barstool back in place. "Next time I'll beat you for sure." Stone dropped two twenties on the table.

"All right." He looked at the bills. "Too much money there." He reached for his wallet in the back of his jeans.

"That's okay. It'll even out next time we have drinks."

Stone waved goodbye and saw Armstrong eyeing another table where two men and a woman were playing. He speculated his friend would be checking to see if they would like a fourth. If not, Armstrong was personable enough to engage with other pool players looking for another player.

Stone stepped out into the cool air. The day had been hot and the weather forecast was for rain. When it came to bad weather, the forecast was always right.

The Metropolitan Billiards Café, usually called The Metro, was a long-established bar, featuring fifteen pool tables, a stage for a band, a dance floor, and a large assortment of beer. Stone liked the friendly atmosphere of the bar, skirting the fine line between being an easy spot to meet people and not being a pickup place. The location, just outside the downtown core, was a short distance from where he lived.

The Metro was quieter than usual. Stone knew the south side of the city was where most of the party crowd had gone. The Fringe festival was a ten-day event and the bars near the theatres did a lively business.

His girlfriend, Cindy, had expressed interest in going to some of the plays. Stone was not as enthusiastic to watch live theatre and suggested a movie instead. The result ended with her making plans with a group of her friends, men and women, to attend some plays. Stone was excluded, making him feel slightly annoyed.

He reached his car just as rain speckled the windshield. He checked the time on his dashboard, judged Cindy would be off in two hours, and figured they could have a drink together. He sent her a text, offering to give her a ride home. *Maybe I've got to find a way to spend more time with her, even if it means going to the Fringe.*

His phone rang. "Stone here. Speak." He listened. "Okay, I'll head there now." *It's going to be a long night.* He sent a second text to Cindy, cancelling his previous offer to give her a ride home.

18

Roberts arrived at the Walterdale Theatre, seeing Stone was already talking to the coroner, Dr. Neelam Hangal. Nearby, a group of people stood, looking at the sheet-covered body. A distressed woman stood staring at the body, clutching a white tissue.

"What happened?" Roberts asked as she approached Stone.

"Looks like murder. Dr. Neelam suspects our victim has been poisoned." He filled in the details of his name and time of death.

"From what? Did he eat something here?"

Stone shook his head. "No, nothing was consumed around here. He's an actor. He and the others just finished doing a play." He pointed at the Waterdale Theatre. "Over there. Ironically, it was a murder mystery."

"Seriously?"

"Yeah, death imitating art."

Roberts sighed at his joke. "Is that where he took the poison?"

"I don't know yet but it seems plausible."

"Who's she?" Roberts pointed at the woman standing with the tissue.

"The victim's girlfriend, Tanya Conner. You may have better luck talking to her than me. She kept crying, so I told her to wait and we'd question her later. The rest of the actors said they didn't notice anything unusual."

"Okay, I'll talk to her."

Roberts walked up to Conner. "Hi, Tanya. I'm detective Anya Roberts. I understand Paul and yourself were actors in a play."

Conner nodded. "*Death of a Philanderer*. Paul was the leading man. He actually played two roles." She used a tissue to dab at her eyes.

"Why don't you come with me? We can sit on that bench."

Conner saw the green metal bench and nodded.

After they sat, Roberts asked, "Is everyone here an actor?"

"Yes. Well, except for Dana Sharpe, who left the play a couple of weeks ago for personal reasons, and Kimi, who's with Mitch."

"Did Paul have any enemies, someone who wanted to do him harm?"

Conner bit her lower lip. "Mitch Donnelly. He was angry when Paul got the leading man role and not himself. Also, at the time, I was going out with Mitch. I ended up breaking off with Mitch and started going out with Paul."

"Do you believe Mitch is capable of murder?"

"He's a loner, temperamental, and smart. It's hard to know what he's thinking at times. I guess he would be capable of murder. I hope not."

"Okay, that's it for now. We'll contact you later. I'll get one of the officers to drive you home."

Roberts spoke to one of the officers and went over to where Stone was writing in his pad. "What do we know?"

Stone conferred with Roberts. "I've collected names and contact information from the rest of the actors. We probably can start letting them go home. Did Conner give you any more information?"

"Not much. She told me of a conflict between Mitch Donnelly and our victim, so we do have a starting point."

"Okay, I'll talk to Donnelly now and then we can call it a night."

———

DONNELLY SLOUCHED ON THE BENCH, THE SAME ONE CONNER SAT on earlier with Roberts. "Yeah, so I didn't like Paul. I didn't kill him though."

Stone pressed forward. "I didn't expect a confession from you. But of everyone in the play, was there anyone else who may have had a grudge against him?"

"You're the detective, find out for yourself."

"Do you really want to play the jerk with me? The guy who can haul your ass downtown and hold you twenty-four hours on suspicion of murder?"

"Fuck. I really didn't pay attention to anyone else who disliked him. I know I didn't do it."

"All right. Keep close to your phone in case we need to call you."

He watched as Donnelly leave the area with Kimi Philips hurrying after him.

"Well?" Roberts asked.

"I think we need to wait for the coroner's report on what poison killed him. Maybe that will help narrow the suspects. Right now, if we assume it was a poison in food or drink, we don't know how it may have been added or by who."

"I don't know anything about the play or how the actors interact, but right now, I'm assuming it could have been anyone. The other thing is they all came from acting in a play. Maybe the poison was administrated before the play started and just now showed its effects."

"Good point. Let's have the theatre where the play was held sealed off until we can take a closer look." Stone yawned. "Okay. Tomorrow is another day."

19

THE CHAIR CREAKED AS STONE LEANED BACK IN IT. "DAMN, THAT was hardly enough time for sleeping."

Roberts answered, "I can agree with you there. So now, we have two murder cases."

"Yeah, with one of them getting a bit cold. Then there's the murder out in Stony Plain."

"That's not our case."

"True, but we can't ignore that it may be related to ours."

"I don't see how they can be connected." She paused. "Are you looking for an excuse to contact her?"

"This is strictly business. And no, there isn't any romantic interest here."

"Okay." She stared at him. "So to clarify, you don't find her attractive?"

"Irreverent." He took a sip of his coffee. "Now, let's get back to work or talk about your personal life."

Anya grunted. "That would be a short conversation." She watched as he punched buttons on his telephone. He pivoted his chair away from his desk, making it harder for her to hear him or see his facial expression. A few minutes later, he hung up.

"The RCMP have a bit more information on the killer."

Anya clicked her pen a few times. "Well?"

Stone smirked. "Now you find the murder in Stony Plain interesting. The RCMP forensics examined the initial blows on the head of the victim and determined the killer was about the same height or shorter."

"Travis Moore was five-nine. If the killer was under that height..."

"It means the killer could also be a woman."

"True. Now how does that relate to our murder case? I'm referring to Jacob Carlton."

"I don't know yet. But there was a red bike parked in the neighbourhood of where Moore was murdered, and a bike was heard on the night of Carlton's murder. Maybe it was the same bike."

"Even if it was, that doesn't mean the bike rider was the killer."

"If it was the same bike, that's too much of a coincidence. Same bike at two murder scenes? Come on, it had to be the killer."

"I'm not convinced one bit."

"I see a connection. I'm not going to ignore these clues."

"Whatever. What about our latest murder? Where do we start with that? Interview the actors?"

"We'll get to them. I thought we should talk to the director and writer of the play, Peter McNab. I would like to know if he has any insight on the actors of the play or if there was a conflict between any of them."

"All right, I'll find out where and when he's available."

———

Stone peered inside Peter McNab's office as he knocked on the doorframe. Cups, piles of paper, and books competed for space on a desk.

McNab looked up from behind his desk. "Are you the detectives?"

Stone nodded and introduced Roberts and himself. He stepped inside the office and noticed a file folder full of paper on one of the two chairs facing the desk.

McNab stood and waved at the chair with the file folder on it. "Please sit down. Just put the file on the desk." He looked at his desk. "The floor would be fine."

Stone studied the file folder. Black ink on the front proclaimed it to be a class assignment from last year. He placed it on the floor, trying to ensure the contents inside didn't spill out on the floor.

"We're investigating the death of Paul Church. Since you are the director of the play he was in, are you aware of any conflicts he was having with the rest of the cast?"

"Well, I certainly don't wish to speak ill of the dead, but Paul did cause a problem that I had to address. He had romantic notions about another cast member, Tanya Conner. At the time, she was going out with Mitch Donnelly, another of our cast members."

Roberts asked, "Did Church and Donnelly get into a confrontation?"

"Yes, at the end of a rehearsal. It was more of an argument between Tanya and Mitch, but it was Paul who was in the centre of it."

"What is Donnelly like? Does he have a temper?"

"Yes, I suppose he does. He's rather moody and normally keeps to himself. However, he does have a rough edge to his personality and does allow his anger to come through."

"Who else may have a grudge against Church?" Stone inquired.

"None that I'm aware of. Of course, being the director and writer of the play, I'm not privy to all the interactions of the actors."

"How about yourself? Do you have any personal feelings about him?"

McNab hesitated before answering. "I found him a pleasant young man in the classroom but I was frustrated at his lack of acting ability when he performed on stage." He interlocked his fingers and rested them on his stomach. McNab leaned back in his chair and spoke in a lecture voice. "Those outside the live arts often don't appreciate the work, the study, and training it takes to be an actor. It is one thing to watch a play and watch an actor repeat rehearsed lines but another for them to put life into those words. Our young actor, Paul, was a good speaker in the classroom, and he certainly had the looks of a male lead. Unfortunately, onstage, those qualities vanished. What we were left with was an uninspiring, monotone repetition of the script."

"I see." Stone watched McNab's face as he asked his next question. "Could his problem be with the play itself, such as a poor script?"

"No! It was a great play, and if I do say so myself, superbly written. The play's failure to garnish more positive reviews lay solely on Paul and the rest of the cast."

Stone closed his notebook. "I suppose it was difficult to have your play end with the loss of Paul Church. I understand the last performance garnered a lot of positive reviews."

"Yes, thank you for that observation." He slowly breathed out. "However, we may be able to revive the play and fulfill the remaining dates."

"Really? Did Church only have a minor role in the play?"

"No, actually, he had a major role and played two characters."

"Won't that be difficult to replace?"

"Actually, I have a replacement that should be excellent in the role. I do have to discuss this with the rest of the cast. However, as the old saying goes, the show must go on."

Stone stood. "Honestly, I didn't expect the play to show again with the death of a cast member."

"As I said, I need to talk to the others first but it's important we do what we have prepared for."

———

ROBERTS ASKED AS SHE RETURNED TO THE CAR, "CAN YOU BELIEVE McNab believes it's okay to just resume the play after one of the actors is murdered? That seems a bit cold to me."

"I guess he has his priorities. I'm just surprised he already has a replacement in mind. Did you see how he reacted when I suggested the play may have been the reason for the weak acting?"

"Yes, he took the criticism rather harshly. Do you think he may have blamed Church for the poor reviews and decided to get rid of him?"

"It crossed my mind. If he does reopen the play, can you imagine the response? People would flock to see a play where the previous leading man was actually murdered. Would those who review plays dare give it a poor review with the rest of the cast bravely carrying on?"

"It could make McNab rather famous." Stone frowned. "He strikes me as man who believes the end justifies the means. How far would he go to ensure the success of his play?"

"Murder might not be too far-fetched. Where to next? I vote for Church's girlfriend, Tanya Conner."

"Your vote carries the day."

———

CONNER'S APARTMENT WAS LOCATED NORTH OF THE GRANT McEwan campus, in a building that held three hundred units stacked in five stories. Stone and Roberts walked down a long hallway, reaching the apartment door. He barely finished knocking when the door opened, revealing a room of mismatched furniture, assorted magazines, papers, and clothing.

"Ms. Conner, may we come in? We would like to ask you a few questions."

Conner nodded, gesturing them to enter. "Sorry, the place is a bit of a mess." Her face looked puffy and her eyes had a red tinge to them.

Stone sat on a love seat after removing a T-shirt from the cushion. Roberts joined him on the practical, yet uncomfortable furniture. Between them and a non-matching armchair, a coffee table held two tumblers. Two diet cola cans accompanied the nearly empty glasses.

"Can I get you anything? I can make coffee or tea." Conner hesitated from sitting in the armchair.

Stone looked at the tumblers. "We'll have whatever you're having." After Conner disappeared into the kitchen, Stone whispered, "It appears she's been drinking and just had a crying spell. I wonder who the friend was that was here."

Conner returned with a milk carton, spoons, and a sugar bowl, placing them on the coffee table. She went back to the kitchen, bringing three mismatched mugs. She sat in the armchair. "Sorry, I'm really out of sorts. I can't believe Paul is dead."

Roberts gave a short smile. "We know this is difficult for you, but we need to ask a few questions." She pointed at the tumblers. "You had a friend over?"

"Yes." She wiped away a tear. "I don't normally drink this early, but my friend suggested I have a couple of drinks and let it all out. So I did and I think it helped."

"Who was your friend? Another actor?"

Conner shook her head. "No, her name is Janet. I've known her a long time and she recently came back from working in New Zealand."

"Did Paul have any enemies, those who didn't like him? Specifically, those involved in the play."

"Yes, there were a couple of actors who didn't like him. And Peter, the director, was angry with him."

"Why was he angry with him?"

"It wasn't fair how he blamed Paul for some of the comments and reviews about the play. Paul didn't have any acting experience before, yet Peter picked him as the leading man with two roles. Paul tried his best but wasn't used to performing in front of a crowd. He had difficulty relaxing and becoming the character in the play. Peter put him in a very difficult position and then berated him for not being a better actor. Anyway, on the last night we found out he may have been planning to replace Paul and perhaps myself."

"How so?"

"Tyler, that is Tyler Burgess, spotted another male actor standing with Peter as we were setting up on the last night. Apparently, this other actor is quite good and had performed in the Fringe last year."

"And you would be replaced as well?"

"We also saw Dana Sharpe there. She initially had a part in the play but then pulled out for personal reasons."

"So why do you think you would be replaced?"

"If Peter took Paul out of the play, I would quit. I think Peter knew that, so he might have contacted Dana to take over my role."

"So, Dana was part of the acting troupe as well. How did she feel about Paul?"

"I don't know. Dana is weird, hard to read what she's thinking. In class, she would sometimes wear a short skirt and a bright top, be flamboyant and drawing attention to herself. She would flirt, laugh, and carry on as if she was the most popular girl in school. Then a couple of days later, she'd wear a baggy sweater and loose jeans, and talk to no one."

"You mentioned a couple of actors who may not like Paul."

Conner looked down at the coffee table. "Yeah, partly my fault. I was going out with Mitch. Then I met Paul, and we were playing opposites in the play and that involved touching and kissing. I fell for Paul and told Mitch it was over."

"I assume that meant Mitch was jealous and angry with Paul, along with you."

Conner nodded. "There was some shouting and swearing."

"What's Mitch like? Does he have a temper?"

Conner leaned back in the armchair and stared at the ceiling before returning her gaze to Roberts. "You may wonder why I was going out with Mitch after I tell you this." She frowned. "Mitch is often moody, can be insulting with his comments, and doesn't care what others think of him. He always dresses casual."

Roberts raised her eyebrows. "Yet, you went out with him."

Conner shrugged. "I was at a low point, I had just broken up with... Well, I was alone. I met Mitch in a bar. He was charming for a change and offered to give me a ride on his bike. One thing led to another. He's the reason I took the live theatre course. I thought it would be cool to be in the same class as him. I think that helped kill the romance. I spent too much time with him and saw what a jerk he could be. Even before I met Paul, the bad-boy attitude had run its course."

"Anyone else that may have not liked Paul?"

"Jessica. When Paul first started taking the course, Jessica went out with him on a couple of dates. I gather she was the one who asked him out initially. He decided to end it with her. He told me she was just too much into herself and decided to cut her loose before they got serious. I guess she never forgave him for dumping her. She's really pretty and probably never had been rejected before."

"What makes you think she still holds a grudge against him?"

"Just some things she would say, like Paul was supposed to reappear as a ghost, so as she was applying some white makeup on him, she said, 'Now, you're a dead man.' She didn't make it sound like she was joking."

"All right, anything else you can think of that can help us find Paul's killer?"

"No. I just can't believe someone would kill him. He was a good man, getting his life together. It just isn't right."

Stone asked, "What do you mean getting his life together?"

"Paul said he had screwed up when he was living in Calgary. He moved to Edmonton to get a fresh start and I could see how he was changing over the last few weeks."

"What happened in Calgary?"

"He was involved in a car accident. A little girl ran in front of his car and he couldn't stop in time. It wasn't his fault at all but he still felt horrible. He moved to Edmonton to get a fresh start."

"Okay, that's it for now." Roberts passed over her card. "If you think of anything else, please call us. Even small details can help a lot."

Conner nodded. "I never met his family, but if you talk to them, let them know he was really doing well here. I hope they'll let me go to his funeral."

"We'll mentioned that to them."

Roberts commented as they left the apartment building, "That helped to identify at least two actors as possible suspects. I also think we need to visit McNab again. It sounds like he wanted to eliminate Church from the play."

"True, although he could just fire Church. Killing him is a bit excessive. One thing I found interesting is that Donnelly rides a bike. Bikes showed up in our other murder investigation, as well as the one in Stony Plain."

"I don't know if that really is something to connect the dots with."

"The killer in Stony Plain, according to forensics, isn't that tall. Donnelly is under six feet."

"That's still pushing it. But, okay, I'll give that a small possibility. A very small possibility."

———

STONE AND ROBERTS MANAGED TO CONTACT DONNELLY VIA HIS mobile and arranged to meet him at Grant McEwan University. He spotted them at the main entrance, giving them a quick nod.

"Is there a place we can talk?" Stone asked. "Privately."

Donnelly hooked a thumb down the hall. "There're some classrooms down the hall." He led the way to an empty classroom, acting disinterested.

Stone looked around the empty room after ensuring the door was closed. He went to the front and sat at the desk at the front. Donnelly leaned against one of the student desks, dropping three books on the surface.

Stone looked at Donnelly acting bored as he rested against the desk. He saw Roberts position herself at Donnelly's side, one row of student desks away.

"You don't seem to be too concerned about Paul's death."

Donnelly shrugged. "Why should I be? He was an asshole. He died. No big loss for me."

"Well, one reason you should be concerned is that you're a suspect."

"Yeah, well, I didn't kill him. He was poisoned, right?"

Stone nodded.

"Well, I would have beaten him to death."

"Really? He was bigger than you."

"I know how to fight. I'll bet he hasn't had a fight since playschool. I'd kick his ass easy."

"That's a lousy alibi. Because he wasn't beaten to death, that means you didn't do it? Sorry, that won't let you off the hook."

Donnelly crossed his arms, not speaking.

"You own a bike?"

"Yeah."

"What type? Colour?"

"A Harley. It's black."

Roberts asked, "Come on, Mitch. Help us with this. You may not have liked Paul but he did have a family and friends who do care what happened. Also, the killer may have been targeting actors. Maybe you're also on his, or her, list."

Donnelly took a few seconds before responding. "Okay, look, I'm sorry Paul is dead. I was pissed off at him but more so at Tanya. I don't have a clue who would kill Paul or why."

Roberts looked at the books he had set on the desk. "You're taking business?"

"Yeah, I figure a business degree will be good to have."

"Why the theatre?"

"Just for the heck of it."

"For the heck of it? You don't strike me as the type who would enjoy live theatre."

"I'm more complicated than I look. End of story."

Stone stood. "Thanks for your time. If you happen to think of anything that will help us in the investigation, give us a call."

"Yeah, sure." He walked lazily out of the classroom.

After Donnelly left, Roberts asked Stone what he thought of him as a suspect.

"I dunno. He doesn't strike me as a poison type."

"True, but if he's smart, maybe he would use poison to throw us off. It surprises me he likes acting onstage."

"Well, as far as I can tell, all sorts of people enjoy acting. I don't think being an asshole disqualifies him from having an interest in acting. Interesting about him having a bike. If it was red, I'd really get excited."

"I still think the bike is a nonstarter in the investigation. Are we supposed to interview every person that has a red bike in hopes they may be a murderer?"

Stone remained silent for a few moments. "I guess you have a point. But since we don't have much more to go on, I'm not giving up on it as a connection."

"Okay, you focus on connections. I'll focus on real clues. In the meantime, why don't we interview Jessica Knowles? She apparently wasn't that fond of our victim."

———

ROBERTS MADE A PHONE CALL TO KNOWLES AS THEY SAT IN STONE'S vehicle. She answered her mobile but indicated she was busy taking classes and wouldn't be able to meet with them until later.

"You do realize this is a murder investigation? Avoiding talking to us doesn't put you in a good light." Roberts used a speakerphone so Stone could listen in.

"Well, I didn't do it. I have nothing to hide but I'm not missing any classes because he's dead. I'll give you my address and we can meet there at four."

"All right. But, just to be clear, next time we want to talk to you, we'll find out where your classes are and haul you out in front of everyone."

There was a moment of silence and then she gave her address. "And just to be clear on my end, if you ever do that to embarrass me, my parents have very good lawyers available." She ended the call.

Stone remarked, "Well, you struck a nerve."

"Sounds like a girl that has her daddy wrapped around her finger."

"We have some time to kill. I know of a good coffee shop close by."

"I'm shocked. You know where there's a good coffee shop? Will wonders never cease."

———

THE ICONOCLAST COFFEE ROASTERS WAS LOCATED IN THE BREWERY District, a dozen blocks west of the downtown core. The industrial setting inside the coffee shop was in harmony with the old brick building that used to house Molson Breweries, originally built in 1913.

Stone and Roberts sat, with Stone having his usual black coffee, while Roberts opted for a latte.

Roberts took a sip of her coffee and nodded her approval as her phone pinged, indicating a new message. She glanced at the screen and discreetly picked it up from the table to prevent Stone from seeing it. She quickly replied to the text message, considered the next text, and sent a returned message.

"What's up? Anything to do with the case?"

"No, just a friend wanting to get together later."

"A date with a new guy?"

"No such luck. Girlfriend."

Stone's mobile rang, saving Roberts from giving any more details from her messages with Cindy, Stone's girlfriend. She listened to Stone give one word replies to the caller.

"Who was that?"

"That was from the friendly people at the forensics department. It turns out Paul Church did die of poisoning and it was likely consumed during the play."

"So he was poisoned at the Waterdale Theatre."

"Right, and here's the kicker. It was fentanyl."

"Fentanyl is added to all kinds of drugs. Church was pretty nervous acting in front of a crowd. Maybe he took something to help calm down and accidently overdosed."

"So maybe it wasn't a murder after all. Tomorrow morning, we need to make a visit to the Walterdale Theatre and see if we can find any signs of drug use."

"Well, at least we can see part of the Fringe, with all that goes with it."

"True, in the meantime, until we find out otherwise, let's assume this is still a murder."

———

JESSICA KNOWLES'S CONDO WAS IN ONE OF THE NEW TOWERS IN THE downtown core, on the twelfth floor that gave a view of the new arena. The detectives were admitted to her apartment by an unsmiling Knowles. She was polite but made it obvious she wasn't pleased with them.

She escorted them to the living room, furnished in white leather chairs, a coffee table made of lacquered wood, and carved wood African artifacts. She sat in a swivel chair and stared at them sitting on a two-person couch with a drink holder in the centre.

"Now, what can I do for you?"

Stone spoke. "You can start by telling us about your relationship with Paul Church."

"We were classmates, and as you know, we both had parts in the play, *Death of a Philanderer*."

"How did you feel about him?"

Knowles frowned. "I thought he was a bit of a fool. Quiet in class. Couldn't act very well. Other than that, I didn't really think about him much."

"I understand you went out a couple of times but he broke up with you."

Her jaw dropped slightly. "Oh, that." She paused a moment. "I felt sorry for him. He was looking lonely, so I suggested we have a coffee or a drink together. I was just being friendly, trying to help him. So we met up a couple of times but he acted kind of funny. I was actually relieved when he said he didn't want to go out with me again. I only went out with him to be nice. I thought it was a bit rude of him the way he ended it."

"But you held a grudge after that, I understand."

She shook her head. "No, I don't waste my time with thoughts about guys like him."

"So, you didn't tell him—" Stone referred to his notebook "—'Now, you look like a dead man,' when you applied makeup to him?"

"Really? I made a joke. He was supposed to look like a ghost. I put white powder on his face and skin."

"Okay, just bad timing for that joke, then?"

"Yeah, whatever. I'm sure neither the powder, nor the joke, caused his death."

"Ms. Knowles, as the stage manager, you were responsible for the set up for the play. Can you tell us who may have had access to where the cups and glasses were kept?"

"Just about everyone in the play. We all mingled around the stage. If there was poison in one of the glasses, I suppose anyone could have done it. I didn't pay any attention to them."

"Okay, but you were the one who was responsible for ensuring the cups were in place at the beginning."

Knowles's eyes widened. "I didn't put any poison in the cups."

Stone nodded. "But perhaps you can see why you're a person of interest."

Knowles looked at Stone and Roberts. Her face blank of emotion.

"Ms. Knowles?"

"I didn't have anything to do with any poison. You have to believe me."

"We don't have to believe anything you tell us but we'll consider what you have told us. In the future, when we contact you for an interview, we expect better cooperation from you. Too busy taking classes doesn't quite cut it in a murder investigation."

"I understand. I'm sorry. If there's anything I can do to help your investigation, I promise I'll do it."

"Anything?"

Knowles answered slowly, as if sensing a trap, "Yes."

"Excellent. Tomorrow morning, we are going to visit the Walterdale Theatre. We would like you to join us and help us understand the positions of the actors and how the glassware was stored."

"I can do that."

"Good, let's say we meet you at the theatre at nine."

She sighed. "I'll be there."

———

ROBERTS AND STONE EXITED THE APARTMENT, TAKING THE elevator to the main floor.

"What do you think of her as a killer?" Roberts asked.

"She looked like a deer caught in the headlights when she realized her situation regarding the poison in the glasses. I tend to think she didn't know how the poisoning was done but suddenly saw her lack of an alibi. Mind you, maybe she was just good at acting. But she was hardly in a position to refuse my request to be at the Walterdale."

"There is that. What if she's the killer?"

"Then I'm hoping she'll say or do something to expose herself. As the killer, I mean."

Roberts looked at her watch. "Time to call it a day?"

"Yeah, I think so. Tomorrow we can check out the Walterdale Theatre and interview a couple more actors."

———

"HI." CINDY SPOTTED ANYA ROBERTS WAITING IN THE BEER Revolution Pub at one of the high round tables. She sat on one of the chairs.

"It's good to meet you." Anya smiled, "Outside of the Craft Beer Market, that is."

"Likewise. Look, I hope I didn't come across as being weird in wanting to meet with you but Moss has talked a lot about you. I was kind of curious what type of woman could work with him so well. Moss is, as you know, hard to figure out."

Anya looked up at one of the TV monitors located around the walls. The monitors showed which of the beers were currently on tap and their prices. "Yeah, he can be frustrating at times. A good man, but how his brain works is a bit of a mystery."

The server came, gave a suggestion on the available draught, and took their order.

"Moss said you're working on a murder that happened at the Fringe."

"Yeah, one of the actors in a murder-mystery play, of all things. It appears his drink that was used during the play was poisoned. So, all the actors in the play are now suspects."

"Really? Another of the actors poisoned him? That seems a little brazen."

"I suppose so. But only the actors and maybe the director were around the stage before the play started. The audience didn't enter the theatre until the actors were ready for the play to start, so it had to be someone involved in the play."

"I love going to the Fringe and I've seen a lot of plays. I even had a part in a play a couple of years ago. But from past experience, I know sometimes you can get in through one of the side entrances." She grinned. "If you flirt a bit with the security guard and tell him you're part of the play, sometimes they'll let you in. It helps if you have an actors card, which I did at that time."

"You're saying that perhaps the killer wasn't one of the actors? The killer may have come through the back door?"

"It's a possibility."

"Thanks. I'll have to look into that." She took a drink of her ale. "Now, let's talk about something other than police work."

"How about men? Can we talk about them?"

"Oh yeah."

20

ROBERTS AND STONE WAITED BY THE ENTRANCE OF THE Walterdale Theatre, acknowledging the officer standing guard. They saw a white BMW M4 coupe parked on the street and Jessica Knowles stepped out. She briefly scanned the area and walked toward them.

"Just so you know, my lawyer advised me not to come here. But I did make a promise, so here I am."

"We appreciate you coming here," Roberts told her. "Contrary to what your lawyer may have said, you're really doing yourself a favour in helping us. You want us to like you."

Knowles eyed Roberts suspiciously after her last comment.

Stone tapped on the heavy wood doorway of the theatre, attracting the security guard. He held up his police identification when the door opened.

The guard, middle-aged and heavy in the middle, greeted them. "Good morning. All is secure here. No one, including the cleaning staff, have been in the theatre area."

"Thanks." Stone led the way down the short hallway to the theatre. He liked the size of the theatre and how the curved seating arrangement allowed for a feeling of intimacy with the stage. The seating rose from the slightly raised stage, affording everyone a good view of a performance. He walked over to the stage, commenting, "This is nicer than I'd have thought."

"Maybe you should go to a few shows with Cindy. You might find that you enjoy live performances." Roberts noted how the stage was divided by a wall fabricated out of thin wood. She stepped on the stage and looked around, satisfied it wasn't disturbed since the last performance, including any cleaning. She held up a hand at the edge of the stage and spoke to Knowles. "Wait here."

Roberts walked around the stage area, memorizing where the props were located, and looking for anything she considered unusual. She spotted Stone pulling out items from a garbage can, bagging some of the items in clear freezer bags. *The fun part of the job.* She spoke to Knowles. "Okay, tell us about the play. I want to know when Paul took a drink or ate anything during the play."

Knowles took a couple of steps from the edge of the stage. "All right, before the play Paul came in drinking a bottle of water. Just so you know, he had something to drink even before the play."

"Is this it?" Stone held up an empty water bottle.

"I think so. Anyway, the play started with Paul and others gathering around. Paul was drinking out of a tumbler first. It's that clear plastic cup." She pointed to a cup sitting on a coffee table, among two wineglasses, beer cans, and a red plastic cup.

Roberts looked at the clear plastic cup, made to look like a glass tumbler. "So, what was he drinking out of it?"

"A can of iced tea."

"Are you the one responsible for adding the iced tea to his drink?"

"Yes." Knowles looked toward the back of the stage. "I opened a can of iced tea and poured it in the tumbler. It was supposed to look like rum or whisky."

"After you added the iced tea, what did you do with the glass?"

Knowles shrugged. "I just left it there at the back, with the rest of the drinks, on a table. I didn't pay any more attention to it."

Stone asked, "Who was around the table after you left it?"

"Well, no one in particular that I recall. Everyone was walking around. The washrooms and dressings rooms are upstairs, and the stairs are just behind where the table was set up, so anyone could have gone back there."

"Did you notice anyone acting different? Anyone staying close to Paul?"

Knowles smiled. "They're actors, so they all act a little strange. Tanya was staying close to Paul, as you might expect."

Roberts asked, "Was there anyone hanging around who was not in the play?"

"Yes. There was Peter, of course. Also, the security guard and the manager of the theatre, although I didn't see him around the stage. I think he went to his office after he said hello to Peter. Then, there was some chick who was Mitch's girlfriend. She didn't hang around the stage, just sat in one of the seats near the stage." She pointed where the audience sat. "Oh, there was some woman who was friends with Tanya, she came through the security entrance and talked to her for a bit. She was here the previous day as well. What was a bit strange was Peter was conversing with two others. One was Dana Sharpe, she tried out for the play and then dropped out for some reason. I took over her part. Peter also had this other actor with him. I don't know his name but Tyler recognized him."

"That's it? No other people helping with the production?"

"We wish we had more help, but we doubled up on duties. For example, if I wasn't onstage acting, I may operate the lights. Tyler made the wall that went between the living room and kitchen. We all helped paint it. The only other person around was the theatre manager."

"Was he around during and before the play?"

"He would come and go. He had to be here at the beginning and end of the play, so sometimes he would watch from the sides."

"We know you weren't particularly fond of Paul. Anyone else who may have disliked him? Had a grudge?" Stone asked as he inspected the wall that separated the two parts on stage.

"Well, obviously, Mitch. Paul took Tanya away from him. He was so pissed after one rehearsal."

"I understand Paul and Mitch almost came to blows."

Knowles frowned. "Maybe. I think Mitch talks big but he wouldn't get into a fist fight with Paul. Paul was a lot bigger."

"Mitch told us he knows how to street fight and he could take Paul."

"He had his chance to fight him during the rehearsal. He ended up storming out instead. Mitch has a mouth on him, but let's say, his bark is worse than his bite. Anyway, after that one incident, Mitch didn't act like he cared about Tanya and Paul."

"You said Mitch has a new girlfriend?"

"Yeah, real quiet. Mitch doesn't treat anyone, especially women, well." She shrugged. "Unfortunately, I had to play opposite him in the play."

Roberts asked, "Tell us about your role in the play."

"I play an aggressive woman. I'm left alone with Mitch and I have my way with him. I kiss him, push him on the couch, and sit on top of him. Mitch didn't like his role. I think he wanted to be the leading man, the part Paul got. But Mitch doesn't have that look of a handsome playboy. He ended up with the role of a nervous, weak man."

"I guess he wasn't happy with his part."

Knowles smiled. "No, but he did enjoy our kissing scene and couch scene, I can tell you that."

"I have no doubt of that." Stone held up the tumbler. "Was Paul's drink filled more than once?"

"Yes, but he refilled it himself."

"Where is the can of iced tea?"

"I threw it in the recycle bin. The iced tea wasn't poisoned. I took a drink from the can before I tossed it."

"Did he drink out of any other cups besides the tumbler?"

"Just a wineglass. At the end of the play, Paul reappears as a ghost. He thanks the audience for seeing our play and takes a drink from a wineglass."

Stone held up a plastic wineglass in a plastic bag. "Like this one?"

"Yeah, Tanya also used one of those."

"Okay, I have both. We can compare them for poison."

Roberts gestured to Knowles. "Can you tell us briefly about the play? Not everyone was on the stage at all times, I assume."

"At the beginning of the play most of the cast were all together around the coffee table, except for Tanya and myself. Tanya was the last to enter."

"Where were Tanya and you before you came onstage?" Roberts asked.

Knowles pointed to the side of the stage.

"That's where the cups were kept. Where was the director during the play?"

"Peter was at the side of the stage but just to wish us good luck. He spent the rest of the time sitting in the audience."

"So, Peter, Tanya, and you were close to where the cups were kept." Roberts looked at the side of the stage.

Stone added, "A rather hidden area when everyone else was on stage."

Knowles shrugged but looked nervous.

"What about the rest of the play? Who was also on the sidelines?" Roberts inquired.

Knowles thought for a moment. "Well, Mitch, Paul, Tanya and I were on stage for the rest of the play. Brenda and Tyler went offstage for a period of time. They played a couple, where Tyler was a professor and Brenda was his student. They were always on and off the stage at the same time. We had a one-minute stoppage between the two parts. We used that time for Paul to change into Harry Rush and to make up a body on the stage. We were all busy during that one minute."

Stone pointed at a table out of sight from the main stage. "Is that where you applied the white powder?"

Knowles walked over to the table. "No, just a table where we kept things like a copy of the script, coffee, and water bottles. I applied the white makeup on Paul in the dressing room upstairs."

"Does everyone share the dressing room?"

"Yes, it's not a big deal. No one completely undresses there. There are men's and ladies' washrooms attached to the dressing room. Paul tried once to put on his own face powder but made a mess of it. I offered to do it as I've worked makeup before for stage performances. We both sat at the table and I used a couple of brushes to apply the powder."

"Let's take a look at the dressing room." Stone led the way upstairs. The dressing room was large and a second doorway led to other parts of the upstairs. He saw the doors to the two washrooms.

Knowles pointed at the long makeup table with the four chairs facing toward it and a mirror that ran along its length. She pointed at the Kryolan container. "That's the white makeup powder I used."

Stone looked at the container, the brushes, and a box of white latex gloves. "Do you wear gloves while putting on the makeup?"

She shook her head. "Not normally. I use a brush to put the powder on, so it wouldn't get on my hands. Paul would put them on as part of his costume. The gloves would make his hands white, and along with his face, he would have a pale appearance of a ghost."

"Anything unusual happen during the play? Someone acting odd?"

"Hmm. I remember the Kryolan lid hard to remove. I'm the only one using it and didn't leave it on that tight last time. And later, Brenda let out a squeal offstage. She found a spider crawling on her sleeve. The audience had a bit of a laugh when that happened. It happened as I was applying the white makeup powder to Paul's face for his solo speech at the end." She smiled. "Paul asked if there was another dead body for Harry Rush to investigate. That brought a few chuckles from the rest of the actors."

Stone peered at the exit of the dressing room. He sighed. "That information doesn't eliminate anyone yet. How about food? Did Paul eat anything?"

"I don't think he brought in anything, like a snack bar, to eat. During the play, he munches on some snacks that were placed on the coffee table. So he cut off a piece of cheese and ate that along with crackers."

"Let's take a look at the snack tray."

Stone and the others returned downstairs to the centre of the living room area of the stage.

"What happened to the snack tray?" Stone looked at the empty coffee table.

"I threw it away after the performance in one of the garbage cans at the back."

Stone closed his eyes momentarily. "Great. More garbage picking." He walked to the back, pulling on a pair of blue latex gloves.

Roberts waited as Stone had disappeared behind the curtain. "Thanks for coming here and helping us."

"Well, I started thinking yesterday how it looked that I may have had an opportunity to poison Paul. I didn't, I swear, but there were a lot of others around who could've. Am I still a suspect?"

"Everyone who was at the theatre still is. But, maybe your decision to help us took you away from the prime category."

Stone returned carrying a plastic bag. "I've got takeout."

Roberts frowned at Stone's attempt at humour. "Okay, that's all for now. If you think of anything else, please call us immediately."

Knowles left, and Stone turned to Roberts. "Well, what does your truth meter say about her?"

"I don't like her, but I think she's telling the truth."

"I agree. One person we haven't talked to yet is the theatre manager."

"Let's go and find him."

———

RICHARD PARSONS WASN'T HARD TO LOCATE. THE DETECTIVES located him in a workshop and storage area at the back of the stage area. The older man was cordial as he used a screwdriver to work on a wood prop.

"How can I be of assistance?"

Stone replied, "Just a couple of questions. How much of the play, *Death of a Philanderer*, did you watch?"

"All in all, maybe half the play. I would check the stage and seating area a few times during the play."

"The play didn't grab your attention?"

"Actually, it looked pretty good but I had work to do. The Fringe is a pretty busy time for us. Almost nonstop plays." He took a breath. "At least until it was shut down because of the murder. The police told us we'd be closed until the investigation was complete."

"Yes, sorry about that. We need to make sure any evidence isn't disturbed."

"Fair enough. I have enough work to do anyway."

"Did you see anything unusual before or during the plays? Anything out of the ordinary?"

"No, I can't say I did. The last play they did was their best, judging by the audience reaction. Other than that, everything was normal as anything can be with actors."

Stone smiled at Parsons's small joke. "Have you been in the theatre business long?"

"Na. I kind of volunteered for this position. I retired a few years ago and was bored. The long and short of it was I decided to help out with the Walterdale Theatre. They pay me but that's not my reason for doing this. I just enjoy live performances and this old haunted building."

"The theatre is haunted?" Roberts asked.

"The Walterdale was originally built in 1906 as a fire hall. My understanding is that a volunteer died during its construction. Later in the 1980s, it was the scene of a murder. We have strange things happen here. Lights going on by themselves and props being moved. I've heard footsteps where no one could be walking."

Stone stood. "Well, maybe you'll have a new ghost here. If you recall anything about our particular murder that night, please call us." He passed over his business card.

Stone and Roberts left the theatre with the smiling security guard wishing them a pleasant day.

Stone started his car. "Let's send the food, cups and the iced tea can for analysis. Nice thinking about asking if there were other people here besides actors. We have at least a couple more suspects."

"Which ones are you thinking of?"

"McNab or maybe one of those actors he was conversing with. If Church is eliminated, then there's a spot for another actor."

"I don't know about that. Kill someone for a spot in a play at the Fringe? There isn't any money for these acting gigs. And why would McNab kill Church? Just because he thought he should be a better actor?"

"Good point. What about Tanya Conner's friend?"

"Why would a friend of Tanya's murder her boyfriend?"

"Okay, stop shooting down every dumb thought I have. I'm starting to lose my confidence."

"Come on, I'll buy you a nice cup of coffee to restore your brain."

"Ah, now you're talking. My brain will soon be functioning normally again."

"For you, normal is rather subjective."

———

ROBERTS AND STONE DECIDED TO LEAVE THE CROWDED AREA OF the Fringe, settling on a restaurant on Whyte Avenue and 106th Street. The Continental Treat served traditional European cuisine. They also made excellent espresso coffees and desserts, which Roberts and Stone indulged in.

Stone put down his fork. "That was delicious."

"I'm glad you liked it. Now, let's get back to work."

"Yes, let's see if Tyler Burgess is available for an interview."

Roberts picked up her mobile. "I'll give him a call."

Stone signalled the waitress for the bill as Roberts spoke on her mobile. "How come I have to pay the bill?"

Roberts covered her mobile with her hand. "Some rule about guys paying when they're with a lady."

"And the lady would be?"

Roberts glared at him. "You're so funny."

———

ROBERTS AND STONE DROVE TO THE NORTH END OF EDMONTON, entering the community of Castle Downs. At 153rd Avenue, Stone turned right and found the address of Tyler Burgess's home, an older bungalow. The exterior indicated it was well cared for, with a spruce tree dominating the small front lawn. He greeted them before they had a chance to ring the front doorbell.

The living room was small, with a love seat, couch, and an armchair facing each other around a coffee table. The furniture, covered in a mix of leather and dark cloth, looked new. Roberts and Stone sat on the couch.

"I made coffee and tea. Which would you prefer?"

"Tea, please," Roberts replied. "And he'll take coffee. Black."

Burgess went to the kitchen. Stone stood, looking around the compressed living room. He ignored the end tables and went to the adjourning dining room. There, he inspected a bookcase squeezed up against a small cabinet.

"What do you see?" Roberts asked quietly as she moved to stand behind him.

"Murder mysteries. Lots of them." He checked a few more books. "Some true detective stories. A lot of dead people are on these shelves."

Burgess returned to the living room, carrying a tray with the refreshments. Roberts and Stone returned to the couch.

"Thanks for the coffee." Stone looked at the coffee cup, featuring a Winnipeg Jets hockey team logo on it. "You're from Winnipeg?"

"No, my girlfriend is. She gave me the mug, knowing they're not my favourite team." He grinned. "She has a sense of humour."

Stone watched Roberts pour milk into her tea mug, decorated by a figure of Donald Duck. She gripped the top of the mug with her fingertips as she used a spoon to stir the contents. "I'm assuming you know why we're here. We're trying to determine who would poison Paul Church. Right now it looks like the poison was administered during the play, likely by food or drink. Any information you may have would be appreciated."

"Honestly, I don't know who killed him or even who would want to. Paul was a nice guy, a bit on the quiet side, so I doubt he offended anybody."

"How about Mitch Donnelly? He seemed to be angry with him."

"Yeah, well, Mitch is a hot-head. He might act out on impulse, like to punch someone. I just don't see him plotting to poison Paul. And for what? Because he stole his girlfriend?"

Stone nodded. "True, that is a stretch." He pointed at the bookcase. "I noticed you're a big fan of murder mysteries."

"Yeah, one of the reasons I wanted to have a part of the play is that it was a murder mystery. I thought it would be a bit of fun."

"Since you are such a big fan of murder mysteries, do you have any thoughts on this murder?"

"Actually, I do." Burgess looked like he was opening a Christmas present. "Paul was like a big puppy. Easy-going, not pushy. He was very polite onstage. At first, I thought he might be gay but that certainly wasn't the case."

"Because he hooked up with Tanya?" Roberts asked.

"Yeah. I may be out to lunch here but I don't believe anything that occurred on the set has anything to do with his murder. Maybe it was something he did in the classroom. He took that live theatre course taught by Peter. But I have a feeling he was also a quiet guy in the classroom. Just speculating. I didn't take the acting classes."

"Which means?" Roberts was wondering why Stone was asking Burgess his thoughts on the crime.

"It means his murder may not have anything to do with him specifically. Maybe he was murdered at random. Like someone put poison in his tumbler but didn't care it was him."

"An interesting theory." Stone remarked. "Let me ask you a hypothetical question. If you were going to kill Paul, how would you do it?"

Burgess sat back in his chair. "Hmm, well, I wouldn't put poison in the cups at the back area. Too much risk of being caught. There's always someone walking around the back. Now, because I'm on the set, I can pick my spot during the play. When the lights go out during the play where Paul's first character is murdered, I'd place a poisoned piece of cheese where his character Detective Harry Rush takes a bite from the food tray. It would be easy to do and without much risk of being caught."

"Interesting, although you'd have to make sure Paul took that piece of cheese."

"True, placement would be important. But there's little danger of being caught."

"Okay, thanks for your time, Mr. Burgess. If you think of anything else, please let us know."

"I will. I have to admit I never expected to be this close to a murder. I'll be looking at my murder mystery books a bit different now."

"What book are you reading now?"

"One about a serial killer."

"More murders for the price of one book. Thanks for the coffee."

Stone reached his car. "You know, maybe Burgess is on to something. Maybe there isn't a motive for killing Church for anything he did during the play. Maybe he was murdered for something he did in the past, or maybe, he's a victim of a serial killer who has a different criterion for killing."

Roberts sat in the passenger seat. "Oh no, don't tell me you think there's a relationship between our shooting victim and Church. What could our two victims have in common?"

"That remains to be seen. I'm just saying it's a possibility to consider."

"Not everything is connected. For example, your thinking and reality."

21

THE FOLLOWING MORNING, STONE FINISHED HIS COFFEE AND watched Roberts as she delicately ate a turnover with her coffee. "If you ate that pastry any slower, it'll be stale by the time you finished."

Roberts paused her eating, took a sip of her coffee, and replied, "Not everyone is blessed with the size of your jaws."

"Thanks for the compliment. However, my point is you don't normally eat as if you have a toothache."

"If you must know, I read an article on dieting last night. It suggested to eat slower and take smaller bites. You eat less and it's easier for your body to digest what you do eat."

"You don't need to lose any weight."

"Thanks, but it's in a woman's DNA to always worry about her weight."

"I suppose so. After you finish your big breakfast, we need to visit that lawyer's office that handled Carlton's drunk-driving charge."

A police officer approached Stone. "The family of Paul Church are here. They would like to ask you a few questions."

Stone instructed the officer to lead them to an interview room.

Roberts watched the procession go to the interview room. The father, she considered, had similar features to Paul. The son, who looked a few years younger than Paul, had looks similar to the mother. The mother, who had a lighter complexion than her husband, appeared weary with red eyes.

She was glad Stone was doing the update to the family. There was a fine line between assuring the family they were doing the best they could to find who the murderer was, while informing them they didn't have a suspect yet. She knew from experience there was invariably the question of why did this happen and a description on how wonderful the victim was. In this case, she thought Paul Church did sound like a good human being, making it all the harder to explain the why.

She passed the time reviewing the case, looking for any insight they had overlooked. Time ticked by, and now the procession was repeated in reverse. Roberts noted the mother had another bout of crying, and both the son and the father showed they didn't restrain from shedding tears.

Stone approached Roberts. "That was not a lot of fun. The family is very close and I didn't have much to say to comfort them. I passed them the name of Tanya Conner and told them she wanted to attend the funeral. They had known about her through Paul. I guess he told them he had found a wonderful girl. The father said they looked forward to meeting her and would send her details of the funeral when it was set."

"Are you ready to get back to work? Or do you need a few minutes?"

"Thanks, but I'm fine. Let's head to the lawyer's office."

———

THE LAW OFFICE OF HENRY STEVENSON WASN'T AS LARGE AS Benson, Kirkman, Ines and Edwards, and wasn't as high up in the building. Stevenson was a tall, thin man and friendly.

After they were escorted into his office, he quickly asked them how he could be of assistance. He listened to their review of searching for a possible murder suspect for Jacob Carlton.

"Yeah, I heard about the shooting, terrible thing. Not good to have that happening in the city. Was it drug related?"

"We don't think so. We were curious if Jillian Cramer, or any of her family, may have held strong resentment against Carlton."

"You would think that they would. Carlton got off pretty easy on the charges against him but Jillian Cramer was quite reserved. She's a remarkable woman. She took her injuries in stride and never showed any anger. Having said that, she was firm in the insurance negotiations. She listed what she wanted, which included the cost of returning to university so she could have a career that wasn't limited by being in a wheelchair. She refused to accept anything less and the insurance company blinked a few days before court proceedings were to begin. I can say with some confidence she simply turned the page on what Carlton had done and forgot about him."

"And the rest of her family?"

"They stayed in the background whenever I was talking to her. She was the strength of her family and they followed her lead." He spread out his arms. "Jillian and her family just don't seem to me to be the type seeking revenge. Certainly, murder is the last thing I believe they would be capable of doing."

Stone stood. "Thanks for your information. If anything, anything at all, comes to mind, please give us a call."

Stevenson stood and held up a finger. "This may be nothing, but a month after the settlement I did receive a call from a reporter who was doing a feature on drunk drivers and their victims. She was comparing the change in the lives from the victims' point of view and how the circumstances affected the drunk driver, if at all."

"Do you recall the name of the reporter?"

"No, but I read the feature she wrote. It was called "Divided Highways: How Drunk Drivers Impact Their Victims." It was a bit of a sad article in that victims rarely get their lives back to normal, while drunk drivers often carry on as if nothing ever happened. A fine, a small jail sentence, and they return back to their lives. The article was carried by *The Journal.* They can likely provide you with the reporter's name."

As they rode the elevator down, Roberts asked, "Do you think that article has something to do with the case?"

"I don't know but I want to find out who that reporter is and talk to her. Maybe she has more information on Carlton. Right now, we don't have any suspects, so anything would be helpful."

The detectives returned to Stone's vehicle. He started the Veloster and made his way out of the concrete parking structure.

Roberts commented, "If this newspaper reporter doesn't pan out with any clues, do we have any other leads to work on? Or does this become your first unsolved murder?"

"No, we will solve this murder. There are more clues out there. We just have to broaden our search to find them. They may not be in the obvious places, that's all."

"Your reverse quantum effects thing."

"What I believe is that the killer has done something else that we can discover, and those clues can be found in our investigation if we search hard enough."

———

AS STONE DROVE THROUGH THE DOWNTOWN TRAFFIC, ROBERTS made a call to *The Edmonton Journal*. After navigating through the switchboard, she contacted the managing editor for special features.

"Okay, I spoke to the managing editor and she said we can come by. She recalls the article "Divided Highway," but the reporter doesn't work at *The Journal* anymore."

"We might as well speak with her. Maybe we'll learn something."

Stone parked his car, and they entered the building through the glass doors. Part of the facade of the original year 1921 building could be seen and Stone briefly looked at the brick partition before proceeding to the elevator.

"Nice old brick wall," Roberts commented as the elevator doors opened.

"Yeah, it is. I was thinking the wall is like people. False front hiding what's underneath."

"I hope that inspiring thought helps us with solving our case." She pushed the button for the fourth floor.

They weaved their way past desks and cubicles, arriving at the office of Karen Gilmore. The blonde woman was tall and had a no-nonsense look to her. She greeted them, stepping around her desk to shake their hands. Gilmore took off her glasses as she sat back behind her desk.

"How can I help you exactly, Detectives?"

"We're investigating the death of Jacob Carlton. I believe he was mentioned in one of your articles, 'Divided Highway'." Stone added, "When you spoke to my colleague on the phone, you said he, the reporter, was no longer working at *The Journal*."

"Actually, it is a she. Her name is Janet Gourneau. I don't have a phone number or address for her but I do have an email address. She went overseas to work and discover the world." Gilmore passed over a large yellow envelope with Gourneau's email address written neatly on it. "I reprinted the article for you. You can get a digital copy as well but it would have the same information. 'Divided Highway' was a series of articles that appeared over four editions."

Roberts asked, "What did you think of the article? Was it accurate or was it over-the-top to generate interest?"

"It was well written and very factual. I know when Janet was writing it, she got quite emotional over it. She identified with the victims. Maybe something happened to her personally in the past."

"Would you happen to have her notes on it? Perhaps there's more information there."

"No, we only have the final article."

Roberts and Stone thanked her and returned to the car.

"I think I'm going to get a cup of java."

"Of course. It's been almost an hour since your last refuel." She took the paper out of the envelope and began to skim through the writing.

Stone drove toward Jasper Avenue. "I think there's a coffee shop on 104th Street."

"Oh shit!"

"What's wrong?"

"There's a connection between two of the murders. I can't believe you're right."

"Everything ..."

"Shut up." She pointed a finger at him. "No one likes an I-told-you-so."

"So Carlton and Church may have the same murderer?"

"No, Jacob Carlton and Travis Moore are the ones connected."

"We need to find this Janet Gourneau."

———

Roberts paused from staring at her computer monitor. "Not much on Janet Gourneau. Her old driver's licence listed her previous address. Other than that, there aren't any records of her. I put in a request for international records but that could take a while. There are a lot of Janet Gourneaus in this world. I sent her an email but it bounced."

"Yes, but our Janet did do journalism. Maybe she has some articles or writing we can find online."

"I suppose you want me to do the searching."

"You're faster at it than me."

"Only because you're always holding a cup of coffee."

By the time Stone had finished his second cup of coffee, Roberts had managed to find a possible lead. *The Nelson Times*, a newspaper in New Zealand, listed several feature articles by a J. Gourneau.

"That could be our girl," Roberts announced.

"Maybe we can give them a call and see if it is her and if they can tell us how to contact her."

"We'll have to wait a bit to call. They're eighteen hours ahead of us."

"Then let's go for lunch."

"Sure. That sounds good. Where?"

"A bit of a gem I found."

———

Normand's Bistro was located in the Citadel Theatre, serving lunch besides dinner for the theatre patrons.

"This is rather nice." Roberts ordered the kale salad and she looked around the open decor of the restaurant.

"It is a nice place to get away from the fast lunch crowd."

"How's it going with Cindy?"

Stone acted surprised by her question. "Hmm, well, a few days ago I was wondering where I stood with her. I called her last night, and she was as sweet as peaches and cream. Women are hard to figure out."

"Men aren't supposed to figure us out. We like guys on the defensive."

"Women are wicked but men like them anyway."

"Don't you mean love them anyway?"

"No, that would imply commitment. Let's not go there." He grinned.

"Jerk." She smiled back at him.

The waitress brought her the salad and his elk burger.

Stone looked at her salad. "Really, take a look at this burger. Are you sure you made the right menu choice?"

"Ask me again when you get your first heart attack."

"Aren't you the tidings of joy." He took a bite of his burger. "If this kills me, then at least I'll be in heaven."

———

THEY RETURNED TO THEIR DESKS. ROBERTS MANAGED TO PUSH THE right series of numbers and connected with the switchboard of *The Nelson Times*. She spoke first with the managing editor of the New Zealand newspaper, who forwarded her call to the editor of special assignments, Andrew Ford. Roberts put her phone on speaker mode, after Roberts had identified themselves as being with a Canadian police department. The managing editor of the New Zealand newspaper didn't ask for any special confirmation of their status as he listened to their request. She assumed he had a call display showing that the call was originating from the Edmonton City Police Department.

"We're looking for Janet Gourneau. We understand she works for your paper."

"Yes, Janet still does work for us on a freelance basis. She is away on vacation at the present moment, so I'm not sure how to get in immediate touch with her." Andrew Ford spoke with what Stone and Roberts perceived as an accent.

"We need to get in with contact her. Do you have a phone number or even her email address?"

"I do have an email address for her. However, her mobile number might not be much of use. She mentioned she was going to Canada and wasn't sure if taking her phone with her would be worthwhile. I will give you her number but I can't promise you she has it with her."

Roberts copied down the information. "One last thing, could you send us a photo of her?"

"I can. Is she in any sort of trouble?"

Roberts looked at Stone, who shook his head. "No, it's just that she may have some additional information on an article she wrote."

"Very well. If she contacts me, I'll let her know that you wish to speak with her."

Roberts thanked him and ended the call. "Now, that's interesting. Our reporter is back in Canada."

"Indeed, it is interesting. I'm going to send in a request to the Canadian Border Security Agency to see when she landed in Canada and where."

"Okay, while you do that, I'll try calling Ms. Gourneau." Roberts tried the number, and after several rings, went to voice mail. She left a message, requesting a return call. She then sent an email, asking her to contact them regarding a newspaper article.

Stone looked up from his desk. "No luck?"

"No, but I left her a message. I guess we wait to see if she responds."

"In the meantime, maybe we can work our Fringe murder. We still need to interview Brenda Thompson."

"True. Why don't you call her for an appointment while I get us a cup of coffee?" Roberts stood.

"Sure, make me do all the hard work."

———

Brenda Thompson informed Stone she would be home at five p.m. and gave him her address.

Stone drove to the north Edmonton location, a four-story condominium. He parked in front of the address and peered at the building. "Not a bad-looking building. Let's see what the inside looks like."

Brenda Thompson showed them in, offering them coffee. Stone, as usual, readily accepted. Roberts declined and looked around the well-lit living room. The walls held a few paintings, including a large Disney print of Sleeping Beauty.

Thompson sat in a pattern armchair across from Stone and Roberts on a couch. "How can I help you?"

Roberts asked, "What do you do for a living?"

"I'm a pharmacist."

"You're also an actor in the play where Paul Church died."

"Yes, I'm taking some evening courses at Grant McEwan. Just for fun. I saw a poster asking for auditions to perform in a Fringe play. The instructor, Peter McNab, was directing a play he wrote, so I signed up."

"But you didn't take his acting class?"

"No, but I understand it was a small class." She paused and lowered her voice slightly. "Even so, I heard that not many in the class wanted to be part of the play."

"Do you know why?"

"Well, this is only second-hand information I heard, but Peter was not a well like instructor. He could be, shall we say, a bit too focused on his supposedly past accomplishments. It would make for some rather tiresome lectures."

"Was Tyler Burgess, besides yourself, the only one not in the class that was in the play?"

"Yes, he was going to help on the play anyway. Tyler is a handyman and built the wall we used on the set to separate the stage. He decided to try acting as well."

"Is this your first acting experience?"

"Just a bit in high school and I was a voice in a radio play once. That was a while back."

"Fair enough. Are you from Edmonton originally?"

"No, I moved here a few years ago. I was an army brat, so my parents moved around a lot, and we lived in Winnipeg for several years. I went to the University of Manitoba and took pharmacy."

Stone nodded. "Okay, did you notice anything unusual during the play? Especially the final performance."

She shook her head. "Not during the play, necessarily. But Peter sat with Dana Sharpe and Marc Crestman. Dana initially was going to be in the play but dropped out. Marc Crestman did acting last year at the Fringe. We were all wondering why Peter had invited them to watch the play. It was as if he expected he would need replacement actors."

Roberts nodded, recalling the same information mentioned before. "Anything unusual happened in the classroom? Anyone upset with Paul Church?"

"There was some tension. Peter was quite demanding as a director. Not everyone handled his criticism well. He tore a strip off poor Paul for not showing enough emotion. Then, there was Tanya, who just couldn't keep her hands off Paul." Thompson lowered her voice to a gossip whisper. "She didn't make it *any* secret they were sleeping together." Thompson licked her lips. "There was also something going on between Paul and Jessica. She seemed to be angry with him. I don't know the reason but she definitely didn't like him."

Stone asked, "I notice you have a picture of Sleeping Beauty."

Thompson smiled, staring at the print. "Yes, I love just about everything Disney. I have about thirty Disney character coffee mugs, and all kinds of knickknacks. The picture is my one big purchase."

"Were you friends with any of the other actors?"

"Friends? No, I can't say that I spent time with any of the others, except in the play. I did see some of them at the campus occasionally but merely said hello to be friendly. I just took my courses and went home after that. I mean they seemed nice, but I was a bit older than they were. I think they liked going to the bar, getting drunk, and being silly. That wasn't for me. A woman these days shouldn't be drinking too much in bars. Men will take advantage of them."

"Is there anything you noticed that may help us find Paul's killer?"

"That Mitch Donnelly. Now, he had a bad temper and he really didn't like Paul. Maybe he did something. I don't know, I'm just saying there was a conflict."

Stone thanked her for her information and left.

————

"What do you think of her as a suspect?" Stone asked.

"Not the type I would suspect normally. Like, she collects Disney stuff, including that print. It seems she has lived alone for a long time, judging by her furniture."

Stone drove his car back the way they came. "She struck me as a bit off. I think she likes drama, and not in the acting sense. She seemed eager to tell us all of the goings on between the actors, including that Mitch didn't like Paul. Ms. Thompson strikes me as a person who enjoys watching others having conflicts but doesn't like to do much herself. I don't see her as a killer."

"She is a pharmacist and thus has access to drugs. She would know about poisons."

"True, there's that. But that's a big leap to actually adding the poison to Church's wineglass or however he consumed the poison."

"So, no suspects."

"Hey, there's a bar up ahead. Want to go for a drink?"

"Sure." She looked at the sign above the bar in the strip mall. The Crown and Anchor looked like it had been around a few years.

It was easy to find a parking spot, and Roberts and Stone opened the heavy wood door. Inside, the interior tried to establish an English-style pub interior. Their server was quick to arrive at their table, giving them a smile and asking if they were interested in the wing special. Stone readily agreed to the wings and ordered a pint of beer, along with Roberts.

"Something on your mind?" Roberts asked.

"This bar, by coincidence, is about halfway between where Brenda Thompson and Tyler Burgess live. Just a thought."

"Brenda said she doesn't like bars."

"She said a lot of things. What she actually said was more that she didn't like to go to bars with her classmates."

The wings arrived and Stone was quick to try one. "These are pretty good."

Roberts took one and nibbled at it. "They are."

"Just so you know, if you insist on slowly eating these wings, you may not get many." He reached for a third wing.

She sighed. "Damn diet." She reached for another wing. "I'll at least drink my beer slowly."

22

THE NEXT DAY ROBERTS DRANK A TEA IN A PAPER CUP, SPINNING her chair as she thought about the case. As she returned to facing her desk, Stone spoke.

"I received a response from the Canadian Border Security Agency." He took a drink of his coffee before continuing. "Our Janet Gourneau, the world-travelling reporter, landed in Vancouver two weeks ago. She had a second ticket to travel to Edmonton ten days later."

Roberts considered the timeline. "So she would be in Vancouver during the murder of Jacob Carlton and Travis Moore."

"Yeah, I guess so." Stone sounded disappointed.

"Well, maybe she'll contact us and give us information on the killer."

"Maybe. Why would she fly to Vancouver, spend ten days there and then fly to Edmonton? She didn't contact her old editor when she was in Edmonton either."

"Maybe she had relatives or friends in Vancouver. Maybe she didn't like her editor at *The Journal*."

Stone frowned. "I don't disagree with what you said but I still consider her a person of interest."

Roberts watched as Stone picked up his phone, punching in a series of numbers. She listened to him talk to the RCMP officer, Roberta

Constantino. He informed her of Janet Gourneau, advising that she may be connected to the murder of Travis Moore. The conversation continued on other topics, including how often she came into Edmonton.

"Planning a date night with her?"

"No, just being friendly to a cop who didn't give me a ticket."

"Okay, just a reminder you're going out with Cindy."

"I'm aware of that." He peered at her. "Why do you care what I do after work?"

"I don't care. But I don't want you to be hurting Cindy by dating other women behind her back."

Stone took a drink of his coffee, his eyes staring at Roberts'.

She quickly turned her attention back to her computer. "I have a picture of Janet Gourneau from our New Zealand paper. I'll forward it to you and print out a copy."

Roberts got up from her desk and went to a far table where two printers sat. *Jeez, Moss was acting like he figured out Cindy and I got together. I better be careful what I say about her. Him and his damn logic and memory can be a deadly combination.* She looked over where he was standing in front of his monitor, looking excited. *Now what?*

"Anya, I've seen this woman before."

"Where, in a bar?"

"As a matter of fact, yes. In the security video from the Dragonhead's Bar. She was there the same night that Jacob Carlton was murdered. That pretty much eliminates her being in Vancouver at the time of Carlton's murder." He pointed at the monitor. "I'll bet she's our murderer."

"You may be jumping to conclusions there. She was there, but is she our killer?"

"I think she is." He gave a shrug. "But I've been wrong before."

"No kidding."

"Why don't you put out an all-points bulletin and see if we can get lucky in catching her."

"Sure." She began working her keyboard.

He walked behind her. "Add she may be riding a red motorcycle."

"Done."

"Excellent. Now, we're finally getting somewhere on our murder."

"The first murder, that is. What about our Fringe murder?"

"I think we should interview Peter McNab once more. He was alone onstage for periods of time. Maybe he was the killer or maybe he saw something we can work on."

———

Roberts and Stone returned to the Grant McEwan campus. McNab kept them waiting a few minutes as he finished up a class, Plays as Literature. They entered the classroom and he gave them a less-than-warm welcome.

"Hello, detectives, what can I do for you now?"

"We have a few more questions for you, specifically on the night Paul died," Roberts stated.

"All right. Unfortunately, I do have the time. *Death of a Philanderer* will not run again this season. The rest of the cast refused to participate in any more shows." He let an exasperated sigh. "They obviously have no interest in taking the craft seriously. It's just fun and games for them."

Stone ignored his whining. "You were at the theatre during the final performance. I need you to think back to that night and see if there was anything unusual. Anything at all."

"Well, it was Paul's best performance. He suddenly seemed to figure out how to act without being intimidated by the audience."

"How about the others? How was their performance?" Roberts jumped in with a question.

"Pretty good. I was equally impressed with Jessica. She did a fine job as stage manager, applied the makeup to Paul, and was believable in her role as an aggressive woman. She was noticeable onstage as well, using her natural ability to attract attention." McNab paused, "Hmm. Tyler and Brenda accurately portrayed the affection between an older professor and his student. Their embraces were quite realistic. While Mitch still showed too much anger and not enough of being a nervous man, he did react well to Jessica during their scene on the couch. And Tanya was also very good in her performance, showing undisguised lust for Paul. That worked well for the play."

"Did anyone have even a minute alone backstage? We know you were there alone, for example." Stone inquired.

McNab puffed out his chest. "I resent your implication. I did not ever consider such a dastardly thing. Besides, I was on the stage only for a few minutes at the beginning to encourage the troupe."

"What were Dana Sharpe and Marc Crestman doing with you?"

"Dana Sharpe and Marc Crestman?" McNab repeated.

"Yes. Is there a problem remembering that little detail?"

"Of course not. If truth be known, they were there as possible replacements for Paul and Tanya. I was going to replace Paul with Marc and I assumed Tanya would quit at that time as well. But after watching that last performance, I informed Marc that I would be keeping Paul on. If you want confirmation of that, you can talk to Marc or Dana."

"Okay. Let's go back to the time you were backstage for that short period of time. Anything you can tell us?"

"No, the actors were all preparing as usual for the play. Some were repeating their lines. I didn't detect anything out of the ordinary. And as I mentioned, for the last performance, I stayed with Marc and Dana, watching the play with the audience."

Stone pulled a photo out his pocket. "Okay, that's all for now. Tell me, do you recognize this woman?"

"I think so. She was at the theatre, watching the play."

"Really?"

"Yes, I believe she was a friend of Paul and Tanya. She was conversing with them before the play started."

Stone began to walk out of the classroom with Roberts, taking quick strides. He called out, "Thanks for your help."

Roberts hurried after him, "Where are we going?"

"To the administration office to see what classroom Tanya Conner is in."

"Wait a minute." Roberts used her mobile to place a call. She spoke for a few moments. "That was Tanya. She's at her apartment. It seems she still isn't ready to attend classes. I told her to sit tight and we'll be there soon." She grinned. "Now, wasn't that smart of me to phone rather than running to the administration office?"

"No comment." He changed direction and headed to his car.

———

ROBERTS OPENED THE PASSENGER CAR DOOR. "DO YOU THINK THIS Janet Gourneau is also responsible for Church's murder?"

"I don't know for sure, but she is now our number one suspect."

The distance from the Grant McEwan campus to Conner's apartment was short, and a few minutes later, Roberts and Stone were at her apartment door.

"What's this about? You sounded like it was important on the phone." She stood, holding the door half-open.

Roberts looked at the flushed face. "Sorry, I didn't mean to frighten you. May we come in?"

"I suppose so. I don't mean to be rude but I'm having a difficult time since Paul died."

"I understand." Roberts placed a hand on her arm and gently led her to the living room. "I want you to sit down and take a look at a photo."

Conner nodded and sat on the couch. She took the photo from Roberts. "That's Janet. What are you doing with her picture? Is she in trouble?"

"We believe she has important information regarding our investigations."

"Oh. But she's okay?"

"Yes. I want you to call her and ask her to come over. It's important you don't let her know we're here."

Conner stared at her. "Why? What did she do?"

"We don't know if she did anything wrong. But we really need to talk to her."

"I don't want to betray her."

"Tanya, she may be involved in Paul's death. We just want to talk to her. She hasn't responded to our efforts to contact her."

Conner took slow breaths. She stood and picked up her phone on the coffee table.

Roberts and Stone listened to Conner's side of the conversation.

"Hi, Jan, it's me." She paused. "No, I'm mostly okay. But can you come over? I just want someone to talk to." Conner gripped her phone. "Love you, too."

Conner put down her phone. "I told her I wanted someone to talk to.

She said she'll be right over. You better not be lying to me about her being involved in Paul's death. She means a lot to me."

"I told you the truth. She *may* be involved in his death but we don't know for sure. One thing is her failure to contact us. This is our only way to find her."

Stone spoke up. "Look, sometimes we talk to people just to eliminate them from our list of suspects. Try not to read anything into this."

Conner nodded. "Coffee?"

"That sounds great."

———

STONE FROZE AS HE LIFTED UP HIS MUG OF COFFEE AT THE KNOCK on the door. Conner quickly opened door and Gourneau stepped inside. She gave Conner a long hug and a kiss.

"Janet, the police are here to see you."

Gourneau looked at the detectives. She hesitated and slowly walked into the living room. "What do you want to see me about?"

"It might be best if we take you downtown for a private conversation."

Gourneau bit her lower lip. "All right. Am I under arrest?"

"No. We just have some questions."

Roberts led the way to the door.

"Did you have anything to do with Paul's death?" Conner called out.

Gourneau turned around. "No. I would never do anything to hurt you. I had nothing to do with what happened to Paul. You have to believe me."

Stone took Gourneau's arm and pulled her out of the apartment. "It might be best if you hold the rest of what you want to say downtown."

When they reached Stone's car, he stopped and pointed at a red motorcycle parked at an angle. A blue helmet sat on the seat. "Is that yours?"

She stared at the bike. "Yes, it is."

He opened the passenger door and then a third door for the rear seating. Gourneau climbed in reluctantly.

"I'd prefer to take my bike and meet you there."

"Not happening," Stone replied. "You have a way of hiding." He looked at Roberts. "Can you get someone to pick up that bike? We need to have it checked out."

"Okay, I'll have it taken to the police garage."

"Why are you taking me downtown?"

Stone answered calmly. "I'm going to prove you murdered three men."

23

Stone and Roberts entered the interview room with Janet Gourneau. Stone stopped Gourneau as she entered the room.

"Before you get comfortable, we need your jacket, gloves, and boots."

"Why?"

"We need our lab to check for something. Hand them over."

"On what grounds?"

"On the grounds you'll sit here until I get a search warrant and then I'll take them."

Gourneau glared at him and took off her jacket and then her boots.

Stone took her jacket, gloves, and boots. He exited the room and, after a few minutes, returned. Roberts and Gourneau were sitting, separated by a functional table designed to handle abuse.

Stone sat next to Roberts. "Do you know why you're here?"

"I was waiting for you to tell me."

"Well, people die on occasion. Some by natural causes and others by decidedly not natural causes. You're here because of the latter. Does that help you figure out why you're here?"

Gourneau shrugged. "Maybe you have to be more specific."

"Just how many people did you kill?" He scribbled on his notepad. "Does Jacob Carlton mean anything to you?"

"I don't know. His name is vaguely familiar."

"I thought a man you murdered would ring a bell. How about Travis Moore?"

"No, not a thing. I've met a lot of people, so maybe he's someone I met once." She eased back in her chair and crossed her arms.

"Okay, how about Paul Church?"

Her arms dropped. "What? You can't be serious. I didn't kill him."

"Why not? You murdered Carlton and Moore."

Gourneau took a deep breath. "You can't prove that."

"That's not a denial."

"It's not an admittance either. But if you think I harmed Paul in any way, you're dead wrong."

"An interesting choice of words. Why should we believe you?"

"Because it's the truth."

"I hate to disappoint you but you aren't a person I would trust right now to speak the truth."

"Screw you."

"Nice. Insulting someone who's investigating you for a triple murder." He stood. "I'm getting myself a cup of coffee. Do you want anything?"

"Water."

"How about you, Anya?"

"Tea."

Stone left the room, leaving Roberts facing Gourneau.

Roberts waited almost a minute before speaking. "Janet, if you didn't kill any of these people, maybe you should be a little more forthcoming with information."

"Whatever I say may be used against me..." Gourneau didn't finish the sentence, crossing her arms once more.

"And saying nothing isn't exactly proving your innocent. Your call."

Gourneau frowned. "Okay, this Jacob Carlton. What happened to him, how did he die and when?"

"He was shot in the west end of Edmonton on August eighth."

"Then, this may be of interest to you." Gourneau produced her wallet and extracted a yellow receipt. "Here, my plane ticket from Vancouver to Edmonton. I landed in Edmonton on August fourteenth."

Anya examined the ticket. "Interesting."

Stone returned, passing a bottle of water to Gourneau and setting down two cups for Roberts and himself. Anya passed the airline ticket to Stone.

"Her plane landed in Edmonton several days after Carlton and Moore were murdered."

Gourneau added, "It's hard to be in two places at once."

Stone sat, drinking his coffee. "You want to keep with that story?"

"It's the truth."

"Then you have a doppelganger. We have your image in the Dragonhead's bar the night Carlton was murdered."

Gourneau looked at him, her jaw slack.

"I think it's safe to say that you lied to us. Want to try the truth?"

"Okay, I was in Edmonton. But you can't prove I killed anybody."

"That remains to be seen." He stood. "I'll be right back."

Roberts studied the nervous face across the table. "Detective Stone is pretty smart. If there's a way to tie you into any of those murders, he'll figure it out." She watched Gourneau fidget with her hands, take a quick drink of water, and resume her fidgeting. "It'd be easier if you confessed."

"I want a lawyer."

"I'll get you one, but it may be a while for one to show up. In the meantime, you may want to consider your options. If you make it easier for us, we can talk to the prosecutor for you."

"I'll take my chances waiting for the lawyer."

Roberts finished her tea. "Tell me about New Zealand. What did you do there?"

"I wrote pieces for a newspaper and waitressed in a bar. I toured around the country as much as I could."

"I hear it's a beautiful country."

"Yeah, it is."

"Why did you decide to move to New Zealand from here?"

"Warmer weather."

Roberts sighed. "I'm just trying to have a conversation with you while we wait. What happened that made you want to leave? I'm sure it isn't a crime to want to leave Edmonton."

Gourneau tapped her fingernails on the table. "I left Edmonton because I needed to get away. I was upset and needed a change."

"Relationship problem?"

"No, that was good. In fact, I almost stayed anyway because of her. But I was miserable and it would have affected us eventually. I left before I became the problem."

"What were you upset about?"

Gourneau stared at her for a moment. "Let's just say I had an anger issue."

Stone entered the room. "Sorry about the delay. I had to check a few things." He pulled out a chair and sat. "You'll be pleased to know I found out a bunch of things. I traced your movements since you arrived in Vancouver."

"Really?"

"Really. At Vancouver airport, you rented a Ford Fusion. According to the car rental company, you returned the car eight days later with approximately twenty-four hundred kilometres travelled on it. That is the distance between Vancouver to Edmonton and back. So what did you do in Edmonton? Don't tell me. I think I can guess.

"You didn't want to use your rental car to do what you came here to do. There was too much of a chance a car with a BC licence plate would be noticed. So you bought a motor bike. No one usually remembers another bike on the road. And if they did, the bike wouldn't even be connected to you. I checked with the original bike owner. He sold it to a young woman with dark hair for cash. The thing is, you never went to the registries office to change ownership."

"I don't have to register the bike under my name for a week."

"True, but you had your reason for never registering the bike. That reason being the murder of Jacob Carlton with a gun and later Travis Moore with a pipe or a bat."

"Prove it."

"There's gun powder residue on your gloves and blood on your jacket sleeves and the soles of your boots. Care to explain that?"

"No. Why would I kill them?"

"Your newspaper article titled 'Divided Highway.' You were angry with them for the hurt they caused. You went to New Zealand to leave it behind but their crimes haunted you. You thought you had a perfect way to kill them and not get caught. But one thing went wrong."

Gourneau crossed her arms. "What was that?"

"Tanya." He pointed toward the door. "She's here. She came to see if you're all right. I talked to her and it turns out you two were very close at one time. So much so, you couldn't resist but see her again. That was your downfall. If you hadn't visited her, we never would have been able to find you. I do have a question still. Why did you murder Paul Church? Was it because of his car accident where a little girl died? Or was it because he was going out with Tanya and you were jealous. I'm sure Tanya would like to know that as well."

"I didn't kill Paul."

"No? You weren't jealous he was going out with your former lover?"

"I wasn't jealous. I was actually happy she found someone. Paul was a good man."

"Yet, like Carlton and Moore, he hit and actually killed someone while driving his car."

"Tanya explained to me it was truly an accident and he showed remorse."

"So that was your criteria. The men you murdered didn't show any remorse after they killed or maimed someone."

"I'm not admitting anything."

"No? I think we have enough evidence to convict you anyway. You can make it easier for us if you want by telling us where the gun is that you used on Carlton. Or the weapon you used on Moore."

"Why would I do that?"

"So I'll let you have some time with Tanya. Heck, I'll even tell her you're not a suspect in Paul's murder."

Gourneau frowned.

"No? Well, let me know if you change your mind." He stood. "I'll tell Tanya to go home."

"Wait. Please let me say hello to her. Please."

"I don't see why I should be doing you any favours."

Gourneau's eyes began to tear. "I just want to tell her I love her."

"Hmm. I'll bet Carlton's parents and family would like to tell him they love him one more time. Actions always have consequences. Your actions may mean never seeing Tanya again and her believing you killed Paul."

"Damn you!"

"Where's the gun? Dropped in a garbage bin? In the sewer?"

The door opened, revealing a man in a dark blue suit.

"You must be her lawyer," Stone announced.

"I'm her appointed lawyer, yes. My name is Spencer Thomas."

"Okay, just so you know, we have blood and gun powder evidence on her clothes pointing to her as the killer of two men. We have motive and all we're looking for are the missing weapons. Even if we don't find them, we have enough for a conviction."

"I best talk to her alone."

Roberts and Stone left the room. A worried-looking Conner got up from her chair when she saw them.

Roberts shook her head. "Sorry, you can't see her yet. Her lawyer is speaking with her."

Conner nodded. "Did she have anything to do with Paul's death?"

Roberts looked at Stone.

He answered. "I don't believe so."

"But she did kill someone else?"

"I'm afraid so."

"I want to see her and offer my support. I still see her as a good person."

"Commendable. We'll consider a visit after the lawyer talks to her."

"Thanks." She sat again, looking exhausted.

"I'll get you a coffee."

THE INTERVIEW ROOM OPENED AND THE LAWYER SIGNALLED STONE and Roberts to enter.

The blue suit spoke. "Are you open to a deal?"

———

THE FOUR SAT AROUND THE INDESTRUCTIBLE TABLE. ROBERTS waited as Stone opened his writing pad, scribbled a note, and asked, "Okay, what's the story here? A confession?"

"My client is prepared to offer a statement, providing she is awarded some concessions."

"Do tell." Stone tapped his pen.

There was a moment of silence as Thomas read from a sheet of paper. Roberts looked across at Gourneau; her eyes were red and puffy. She was clutching a wad of tissues.

"Ms. Gourneau is willing to make a statement concerning the death of Travis Moore, providing you would tell the prosecutor of her great cooperation. She will divulge the location of the weapon used and details of their altercation." The blue suit cleared his throat. "She also wants you to inform Tanya Conner that Ms. Gourneau is not a suspect in the death of Paul Church. Ms. Gourneau also wants fifteen minutes with Ms. Conner."

"Interesting." Stone responded. "So, your client is willing to admit killing Travis Moore but not Jacob Carlton? I'm not sure, in good conscience, I can say she isn't a suspect in Paul Church's death. I tell you what. If your client will admit to also killing Jacob Carlton and provide the location of the gun used, I will give her fifteen minutes with Tanya Conner. And I will tell her she is not under suspicion of the murder of Paul Church."

"Could I have a few more minutes alone with my client?"

"Why not?" Stone stood. "It's time for another coffee anyway."

CONNER WATCHED STONE AND ROBERTS LEAVE THE ROOM, QUICKLY moving toward them. "Well, what's going on?"

Stone spoke to Roberts. "I'm getting a coffee. You tell her that her friend will be going away for a long time."

ROBERTS WATCHED THE BACK OF THE DEPARTING STONE. "THANKS, that'll be fun." She touched Conner on the arm. "Tanya, I have some difficult news for you. It appears Janet is ready to confess to killing two men, Jacob Carlton and Travis Moore. She'll be going to prison for a long time."

Conner took several deep breaths. "But she didn't kill Paul?"

"We don't believe so."

"Can I see her?"

"Maybe. It depends on what she and her lawyer agree to tell us."

"Okay. I don't know what I'm feeling right now. I'm relieved she didn't kill Paul but worried about what will happen to her."

Stone came back with a coffee just as the interview door opened.

Thomas poked his head outside the door. "I think we can come to a deal."

Once the four sat around the table, Thomas initiated the conversation.

"Ms. Gourneau will agree to provide the location of the gun as well as the weapon used on Travis Moore. She will sign a confession to committing the murders. In exchange, she wants those fifteen minutes with Tanya Conner. Plus, the assurance that she is no longer a person of interest in the death of Paul Church."

Gourneau blurted out, "I didn't have anything to do with his death. I swear."

Stone asked, "So she will confess to two murders?"

"Yes. I informed her the two murders will likely be served concurrently and thus not increase actual prison time. Her cooperation will also help reduce sentencing time."

"Fair enough. After we have her statement signed, she can see Tanya. But first, tell me about your killing spree."

Gourneau bit her lower lip, released it, and spoke in a rush. "When I was in New Zealand I kept thinking how these drunk drivers kill people without hardly any repercussions. If you knife someone to death while you're drunk, you get years in prison. Kill someone in a car, a fricking suspended licence and a fine. I thought I knew how to serve justice without getting caught.

"I bought a gun in Vancouver. It's not hard to find one if you know your way around shipyards and I figured them out in Auckland. I rented a car and drove to Edmonton. I bought a bike for cash and used that instead of the rented car. The bike wasn't registered to me, so I figured I could ditch it afterward and it would appear I was never here. I looked up where Carlton lived and followed him for a couple of days. I caught him walking home one night and shot him." She shrugged. "I ditched the gun in a sewer through a grate in the sidewalk. I didn't want to use the gun again. The same gun could connect me if I used it on Moore, so I used pepper spray and an iron bar on him. He let me into his house, leering at me. I sprayed him and then I used the iron bar on him. I hesitated with the first hit, but I thought of what he had done, and that was enough for me to finish him. I tossed the bar at a rest stop on my way back to the city."

Stone wrote in his notebook. "Do you feel guilty about what you have done?"

Seconds passed. "I feel bad for Carlton's parents and family. When you said they were upset that he had died, I realized there are no right ways to fix what he had done. I screwed up my life. Hurt Tanya. All because I couldn't stop thinking of revenge. I wish I could turn back the clock."

———

Roberts glared at Stone. "So, I have to supervise Tanya and Janet when they get to spend fifteen minutes together, separated by a table, hold hands and say nice things to each other. Meanwhile, you will sit at your desk drinking coffee."

"Essentially, yes. I would sit in but probably some sort of protocol requires a woman to watch two women say goodbye."

"Yeah, makes sense. You'd probably find it interesting. So while I'm on guard duty, maybe you can start figuring out who murdered Paul Church."

"Hmm, there is that loose detail."

24

ROBERTS EMERGED FROM THE INTERVIEW ROOM. BEHIND HER, Janet Gourneau was led away in handcuffs by two police officers. A tearful Tanya Conner stood in the doorway, looking unsure where to go.

Stone stood from his desk and met Roberts. "Everything go okay?"

"I'll tell you later." Roberts turned toward Conner. "I'll get someone to drive you home. We'll be in touch later."

Roberts signalled for one of the uniformed police officers, asking her to drive Conner home. She eased into her five-wheeled chair and pointed a finger at Stone. "You owe me. Supervising two crying women for fifteen minutes? That was torture."

"Did you learn anything?"

"Yeah, love is blind. Tanya still loves Janet, even though she knows she's a murderer."

"Is she going to wait for her until she gets out of prison?"

"No, I doubt it. I think Tanya wants more of a traditional man-woman relationship. She wants to stay friends with Janet. After what happened to Paul, I think she will avoid any close ties for a while."

"Tanya was pretty sure Janet never murdered Paul. Any chance she was so sure because she knows who did? Even herself?"

"Well, the first suspect in a killing is usually the person closest to them." She tapped her finger on the keyboard of her computer. "Hey, we have the results from the water bottle, the food, and the glassware."

"All right, that'll help with the investigation. Which one had the fentanyl in it?"

"None."

"What the... Shit, how did he get the fentanyl in his system? The air? Something he ate when no one was watching?"

"Good question. Maybe we need to make a return visit to the Walterdale Theatre and take a closer look."

Stone stood. "Let's get going. Traffic is not going to be fun at this time."

"Don't you dare complain to me after making me sit with Janet and Tanya."

"Point taken."

———

RICHARD PARSONS LET THEM IN THE DOORS TO THE STAGE AND seating area, apologizing that the security guard went home early with a cold. "It's still the same as the last time you were here. As you instructed, we're keeping everyone out of the theatre area."

"Thanks. Did anyone try to get in?" Roberts asked.

"Not as far as I know. Lots of curious people looking at the yellow tape across the entrance, but that's about it."

Stone and Roberts walked around the stage, checking for any drink containers they may have missed, as well as food wrappers.

He examined the temporary wall that went between the living room and kitchen. "I was thinking that if Tanya wanted to kill Paul, and I can't think of any reason why she would want to, she would be the most likely person to give him a candy or breath mint before or during the play. He would take whatever she offered without question."

"True, she would have the means. But, as you point out, why?"

"There are more questions than answers in this murder." He looked at the prints attached to the temporary wall. "Hmm, these pictures are held on to the wall by two-sided tape, not nails."

"Must be strong tape. Burgess built the wall. He must have used some commercial product."

"Interesting, but not the source of our poison." He wandered through the kitchen, looking around at the fake cupboards and floor area. He heard Roberts walk behind the stage area and heard her climb the stairs to the dressing room. Stone continued his inspection of the stage and went to the bottom of the stairs. He called out, "See anything?"

Seconds passed. "Maybe. Come and take a look at this."

Stone jogged up the stairs to where Roberts stood at the makeup table. "What did you find?"

"This." She pointed at the Kryolan white powder container. "Jessica Knowles used this to put a white face on Paul Church. Maybe the fentanyl is in there."

"Could be. The skin would absorb the drug. Just a small amount could kill him."

Using latex gloves, Stone bagged the container and the brushes. "Let's send this to the lab."

"Knowles was using the powder to apply it to Church's face."

"True, and if this powder contains fentanyl, then Knowles will jump the queue to be our number one suspect."

They returned to Stone's vehicle and headed back downtown to send the Kryolan container to the lab for analysis.

Roberts asked, "What are your plans for tonight?"

"Not something I want to do, but probably the right thing to do. I'm going with Cindy to a Fringe show."

"Really? That's a bit of a sacrifice on your part."

"Well, I think there's something going on with her. I can tell when people are lying to me. She's not lying to me but I sense she's holding back on some things."

"Like what?"

"She went to Beer Revolution, meeting up with a friend. I asked her who the friend was and she just said it was a girlfriend. Not a big deal, but she avoided identifying her friend, never told me her, or his, name."

"I think you're looking for a problem that doesn't exist. Cindy wouldn't go around your back and see someone else."

"You may be right." He looked at her. "What makes you so sure of her character?"

Roberts looked out the passenger window. "Nothing in particular, just how you described her in the past."

25

ROBERTS CARRIED A THERMOS OF TEA TO HER DESK AND SAW STONE was already at work.

"Hey."

He looked up. "Good morning. I just finished up the report on Janet Gourneau and now it's up to the prosecutor's office to determine how to proceed."

"Good." She took a drink of her tea. "When did you get here that you had time to do that report? And why are you so damn cheerful? Wait, you had a date with Cindy last night." She grinned. "I'll bet it was a very good date."

"None of your business, Anya. I just happen to be normally a cheerful person in the morning."

"Since when, *Mr. don't talk to me until I've had three cups of coffee.*"

"Shall we return to the case on hand? Or do we talk about what you did last night?"

"I watched TV with popcorn and a glass of wine. Do you want more information, like which movie or the type of wine?"

He stood. "Spare me the details. I shall get another coffee. Why don't you contact Ms. Knowles and arrange an interview time."

"What if the lab results come back negative for fentanyl?"

"We still talk to her. One of those involved in the play is our murderer and we might as well start with her."

———

Stone parked in front of the condo building, directly in front of the 'No Parking sign'. "Okay, let's go and visit our prime suspect."

Roberts exited the car and answered her phone as she entered the building.

Stone held open the glass door for her as she talked.

"Okay, what was that all about?"

"The lab confirmed it. Fentanyl was in the Kryolan container. We have the method of murder."

"Great."

"Unfortunately, the fingerprints on the can are all smudged. There's a set of small prints around the can, likely Knowles, but any other sets are smudged."

"Let's work with what we've got, then."

———

Knowles greeted them at her apartment, "Hello again, detectives. Please come in." She stepped back and closed the door. "Coffee, tea?"

"No thanks." Stone sat in one of the white leather chairs. "We are looking for the way poison was administered to Paul. It turns out it wasn't by the ingestion of any liquid or food we found. But we are suspicious of the Kryolan container. It would be easy to mix fentanyl with the face powder."

Knowles shifted in her chair. "I see. If there's fentanyl in the powder, then you would suspect me. Isn't that right?"

Roberts leaned forward in her chair. "Not exactly, just a person of interest. Perhaps you didn't put the fentanyl in the powder and merely applied it to Paul."

"I can tell you right now, I didn't put any drug in the powder. Hell, I don't use any of that stuff."

Stone shrugged. "Yeah, but that doesn't mean you couldn't obtain some of it. You have money and connections. You can get pretty much what you want."

"I didn't do it."

"Okay. So you didn't do it. Who else had the opportunity to add fentanyl to the powder?"

"I don't know. I thought that would be your job. But have you considered Mitch? He likes acting like a gangster. He probably has a way to buy drugs."

"No doubt he does." Stone scribbled in his notebook.

"Dana Sharpe. She looked like she was on something half the time." Knowles added, "Also Peter. I know the look of men when they want something. And the look when they're users. Peter was a user, I'll bet on it. Maybe he used a supply of his drugs to eliminate Paul."

"I suppose that's possible. But tell me one reason why we should believe you didn't do it."

Knowles stood. "Look at me. I can get just about any guy I set my sights on. Paul dumped me. True. I was pissed off at him. True. But to kill him for that? That's would be crazy and I'm not crazy. I already have two dates with two different people this weekend. I'm sad Paul is dead. I had absolutely no desire to see any harm to him."

Roberts looked at Stone, who gave a raised eyebrow. "Okay, let's go back to the Kryolan container. Did you notice anything unusual about it?" He flipped the pages of his notebook. "You said the lid seemed to be on tighter than normal."

"No, not the powder, or where the container was. But, yes, the lid was on tight. I leave the lid a bit loose and I'm supposed to be the only one needing to use it."

Stone looked at another part of his notes. "Do you wear gloves while applying the powder?"

Knowles shook her head. "No, the gloves on the table are size large. Paul wore them for his ghost appearance. They're too large for me." She held up her right hand. "All I was doing was adding white powder to his face and it wasn't worth the trouble wearing gloves."

"Was anyone else wearing gloves during the play?"

"No, there wasn't any need to. Paul was the only one wearing stage makeup."

"Was there anyone else around while you applied the makeup?"

"Tanya and Tyler."

"It must have been crowded in there."

"I know why Tanya was there. She was being protective of Paul and didn't like me. I don't know why Tyler was there. I think he was curious if we would get into a fight. Brenda and he loved it when there was a conflict and were always poking in their nose when there was an argument. Tyler loved telling us Peter had brought in Dana and that other actor to replace Paul and Tanya and then watching our reaction."

"Okay, thanks for your cooperation." He closed his notebook and slipped it into his jacket pocket.

Roberts asked as they descended in the elevator, "You don't think she did it?"

"No. If she was the one who put the fentanyl in the powder, why wouldn't she wear gloves and risk being poisoned herself? We can confirm that she wasn't wearing gloves when we talk to Tanya."

"Okay. There was only one pair of gloves in the garbage anyway."

"I think our killer brought in their own gloves to handle the container and, rather than put the gloves in the garbage where their prints would be discovered, carried them out hidden in their pocket."

The elevator doors opened. Roberts used her phone to call Conner.

"She's home?"

"She is. If she can confirm Jessica Knowles wasn't wearing gloves, then we can likely eliminate her as our murderer."

"What about Conner as a murderer?"

"I thought about it. She must be a great actress to look so upset all the time. But there just doesn't seem to be a motive. If she wanted to dump him for Gourneau, she didn't have to kill him."

"I agree. I don't see her as a murderer. My woman's intuition tells me she isn't our suspect."

"There's no such thing as a woman's intuition."

"My woman's intuition tells me you're a trustworthy man."

"Okay, now I'm a believer."

———

Conner opened the door and led them to the sitting area of the living room.

Stone commented, "You tided up your place."

"Yes, I decided I need to get on with life. It was either that or become an alcoholic. I know Paul would not have wanted me to go there. I didn't know him that long but he left a big impact on my life."

"I have a question concerning the play. Jessica applied the white powder on his face in the dressing room while you were there?"

"Yes."

"Did Jessica wear gloves while she was applying the powder?"

"No, she just used brushes."

"Tyler was there as well at the time?"

"He was. He appeared just to be snooping around. He didn't say or do anything."

Roberts and Stone left.

"Now where?" Roberts asked.

"Dana Sharpe. I want to confirm a couple of things with her."

"I'll call her and see if she's home."

———

Sharpe opened the door to the detectives. The small home in the community of Jasper Place was built in the 1950s and featured dull brown stucco on the small bungalow.

"Ms. Sharpe, we have a few questions concerning the death of Paul Church. May we come in?" Roberts showed her police identification.

"Sure, come on in." Sharpe acted happy. She wore yoga pants and short top, twirling as she made her way to the living room. She literally jumped onto the couch, stretching out on the brown fabric cushions. She gestured at the love seat across from her for the others to sit. "Can I get you anything? Coffee? Something stronger?"

"No, thank you." Roberts sat next to Stone on the love seat. "On the night of the last play, you sat with Peter McNab and Marc Crestman."

"Yup, I remember that."

"Before or during the play did Peter, Marc, or you leave the seats? Even for a minute?"

Sharpe rotated on the couch, putting her feet at the opposite end. "No, we stayed pretty much together during the play. At the end of the play, Peter went to the stage to take a bow with the rest of the cast."

"Just at the end."

"Before the play started he went onstage to talk to the cast. I could see him and the rest standing around him. He made a little speech and came right back to where Marc and I were sitting. So I pretty much saw him the whole time. At the end, he climbed onto the stage at the front, took in the applause, and returned to his seat."

"Did he say anything?"

"Just that he didn't need Marc or me for the play. He thought the actors finally managed to get their acting right. Of course, that changed later when Paul died. Who would've thought that? Anyway, he contacted us again a few days later to see if we'd be interested in reviving the play. That didn't pan out as the others didn't want to continue." Sharpe shifted on the couch and sat cross-legged.

"Okay. We're looking for someone who wanted to see Paul dead. Any thoughts?"

"I dunno. Paul was a good-looking guy. Nice to talk to. Someone jealous of him? Maybe Mitch. I'm just guessing." She stood, stretched, and leaned back.

"All right, thank you for your help."

"Hey, I was about to do a yoga routine. Care to join me?"

"Can't. Police work to do."

"Okay. See ya."

Roberts looked at Stone. "Well, that was an interesting talk."

"I would say so. I was wondering if she was going to stand on the coffee table and do a dance. She is one hyper girl."

"Move your mind back on the case. She said Peter and Marc never left the seats long enough to add fentanyl to the makeup powder."

"If that's true, that means we're down to just a few suspects."

"Tyler Burgess, Brenda Thompson, Mitch Donnelly, Tanya Conner, and Jessica Knowles. Which one do you think did it?"

Stone smiled. "That is the wrong question. Let's go back to the Walterdale Theatre."

Roberts gave him a puzzled look. "What do you mean 'That's the wrong question'?"

"I'll explain later."

26

RICHARD PARSONS WAS SURPRISED TO SEE THEM BACK. "MORE clues to look for?"

Stone answered, "Yup, and it may be a big one."

"Good luck, then." Parsons wandered off.

Roberts trailed Stone as he made his way to the men's dressing room. "Okay, what gives? What are *we* looking for?"

"A container of Kryolan powder."

"But we turned the one can in to our lab."

"Let's assume we wanted to kill Church using the face powder with fentanyl. We could bring the fentanyl here into this room, open the Kryolan container, carefully mix in the drug and then put the lid back on. That would take time and anyone could walk into the room and catch you in the act. It's a bit risky for the killer I have in mind."

"Which is?"

"All in due time." Stone used a small flashlight to look behind the furniture. "There's another method to put the fentanyl in the powder. You could buy another container of the face powder, add the fentanyl, bring it here, and swap it for the clean Kryolan container. The swap would be very quick and easy."

"True. So you're looking for another Kryolan container."

"I am. Our killer wouldn't have tried to take it out. A murder happened just after the final performance and they wouldn't want to be caught with that incriminating evidence. You would do the swap right when you first arrived for the performance but wouldn't want that bulky can on your person during the play."

"Okay, that's all convincing in theory. But you don't have the second container."

"Not yet." He went upstairs to the dressing room and looked under the table where the white powder was applied. "Oh no?" He reached up and pulled down a metal can. "Here it is. It was stuck on the bottom of the table by two-sided tape and we know who uses that product."

"Tyler Burgess."

"Right."

She looked at his pleased expression. "Okay, I'm going to assume you suspected him before."

"I did. He wasn't just a murder mystery reader enthusiast. He wanted to try to commit the perfect murder."

"And he obviously failed. But why did he want to kill Paul Church?"

"He didn't have a reason to. No motive whatsoever. That was part of his *perfect murder*. He wouldn't be seen as a suspect."

"So can we prove he did it?"

"I think so. Burgess wore latex gloves, I assume, because he wanted to be protected from the fentanyl and to prevent his fingerprints from appearing on the can of Kryolan. Now, it is true the fingerprints on the can laced with fentanyl only had smudged fingerprints. But this can is different."

"How so?"

"To stick this can under the table, he would have to push up on the bottom of the can. Even if he was wearing latex gloves, a finger print will appear. Did you know that fingerprints can be made even through a latex glove?"

"I did. TV shows always have the crooks wearing gloves, but fingerprints can still show through. You said earlier I asked the wrong question. What did you mean by that?"

"You asked which one I thought was the killer. It wasn't one person. Burgess had help from his girlfriend, Brenda Thompson. She works as a pharmacist and supplied him with high-grade fentanyl. Thus, she was part of the murder, too."

"How do you know she's his girlfriend?"

"His coffee cups. One is a Disney character, and we know how she loves Disney stuff. He isn't the type to collect cartoon figures. The other mug was of the Winnipeg Jets and she went to the University of Manitoba in Winnipeg. They also live the same distance from the Crown and Anchor Bar, likely a place they met. They wanted excitement in their lives and decided a perfect murder would be just the ticket."

"Congratulations. You solved a murder without using your funny quantum thingy."

"A rather strange compliment."

"I'll get our suspects picked up."

27

ROBERTS POINTED AT ONE OF THE INTERVIEW ROOMS. "THOMPSON is in there. Burgess is in the room down there." She swung her hand to the hallway.

Stone took a drink from his coffee. "Which one first?"

"Burgess."

"Okay, you lead, I'll follow."

They sat across from Burgess, who looked agitated with sweat beading on his forehead.

"Mr. Burgess," Roberts began, "we have your fingerprints on the container of Kryolan and that pretty much is all we need to convict you. You do have a couple of options still. We can charge you with murder in the first degree, which entails you planned and completed everything in poisoning Paul Church. You will receive the maximum penalty for that."

"What do you mean I have an option?" Burgess's voice squawked out.

"Tell me where you got the fentanyl from. Did you have an accomplice? If so, then the murder charges can be changed."

"Brenda helped me get the fentanyl. I bought another Kryolan face powder and she mixed in the fentanyl."

"Then you swapped the containers of Kryolan at the Walterdale."

"Yes, but she was the one who added the drug, so she was the one who actually killed Paul."

"That's a bit of convoluted logic." Roberts looked at Stone. "Shall we talk to the other murderer?"

"We need to do that." He spoke to Burgess. "You are one sick puppy, killing someone only for the fun of it."

Roberts and Stone entered the room where Brenda Thomson waited, clutching a tissue.

Roberts sat. "Brenda, we had an interesting conversation with Tyler Burgess. Is it true you added the poison to the face powder container and later changed that container for Jessica Knowles to put makeup powder on Paul's face?"

"No, I only mixed the fentanyl with the powder. Tyler did everything else. It was his idea to murder someone. He said he had a perfect plan not to get caught."

"Why did Tyler and you decide to kill Paul? Was it something he did?"

"No, we didn't really know any of the actors. It wouldn't have mattered which one of them died."

"Why did you want to see one of them dead?"

"We thought it would be interesting to see their reaction. I don't want to sound callous, but those actors were all so young and rather annoying. Always texting, going to bars, laughing at some silly thing on their phones."

"That's why you murdered Paul? Because he was annoying to be around?"

"Well, Paul was better than most. Still. It didn't really matter to me who died. Just remember, it was actually Tyler's idea. So he should take the blame for the murder, not me."

"I'm afraid the judge may see that a little differently."

———

"Okay, the report has been sent to the prosecutor's office."

Stone looked up from drinking his coffee. "Nice work on the

interviews. I thought Burgess was strange wanting to plan the perfect murder but Thompson was a real piece of work."

"They were both willing to throw the other under the bus."

"Not a solid relationship, but they do deserve each other."

"What are you up to tonight?"

"I'm meeting Cindy for a drink at the Local Pub. How about you?"

"Nothing much. I'm going to visit Tanya Conner. I want to tell her personally what happened to Paul. She shouldn't hear it over the news."

"Good point. Do you want me to come with you?"

"No, I think it may be best for me to do that by myself. You're not much for a crying woman."

"You know me well. Say, do you want to join Cindy and me later?"

"What, I thought you never wanted me to meet Cindy."

"Not without me present. But, she's my girlfriend and you're my partner and my friend, so I think it would be good if you at least met her."

"Great, I'm looking forward to it."

Conner offered a coffee to Roberts. "Thank you for coming over. You said over the phone you had news about Paul's death."

"Yes, the murder was committed by Tyler Burgess and Brenda Thompson." She went on to explain how the murder was committed and expressed her own sadness about it not having been done for any rational reason.

"I feel so empty. I lost Paul to a senseless murder and my best friend, Jan, because she is a murderer."

"Is there anything I can do for you?"

"No, I guess I need time to sort things out. I'm going to visit Jan while she's in prison. I know what she did was wrong but I know underneath, she's a passionate, caring woman. But I'll be seeing her only as a friend. I made it clear to her that was as far as I could go into a relationship with her."

"That's wise." Roberts knew the women's prison was located on the west end of the city, making visits easy for Conner.

"Jan told me I need to find a place where Paul and I used to go and have a final drink with him. She said that will help me say goodbye and give closure. I think I know of the place. Paul's family sent me the information about when and where the funeral is. It's in Calgary but I will make the trip. It'll be good to meet his family and I'll tell them what a great person he was."

"Good for you. Take care, and don't be scared to talk to someone about what you've been through. The police have a victim's service that you can call if you want to talk."

"Thanks. I think I'll be okay now."

Roberts left and made her way to her car. *And now for my date with Moss and Cindy. What possibly could go wrong?*

28

"Mr. Parsons, thank you for letting me in."

"Not a problem, Tanya." He led her to the stage, pausing at the side of a curtain to flip a couple of switches to turn on the lights. "You can call me Richard. Take your time, nothing is going on here today. When you're done, I'll be in the back. You can leave the lights on, I'll take care of them later."

Conner watched him disappear and went to a chair near where the kitchen table from the play still stood. She sat, pulled out a small wine bottle from her purse, and a plastic cup.

She licked her lips, taking in a slow breath. "Okay, Paul, I hope you can hear me. It feels a little strange to talk to just the air around me but you still feel real to me." Conner poured the wine into the plastic cup.

"Before you go to where you go to next—" she gave a small giggle "— wherever that is, but I'm sure it'll be a wonderful place, I want to tell you how much I love you. You were the one for me and I'll never forget you." She drank a portion of the wine. "I hope we will meet again and I can tell you again how I feel about you." She consumed the rest of her wine.

"I wanted to have one more drink with you. Don't forget me and how much I love you." She stood and deposited the wine bottle in a recycling bin and the cup in the garbage. "I hope you heard me. Goodbye, Paul. Until we meet again." She blew a kiss into the air.

Parsons looked up from behind his desk. "You're done?"

"Yes, thanks again for indulging me. It meant a lot to me."

"Not a problem at all." Parsons escorted her toward the exit, passing by the stage. "I see you turned off the lights."

Conner looked at the dark shadows across the stage floor. "No, I didn't."

Parsons raised his eyebrows. "I guess we have another ghost visiting the theatre."

THE END

———

Don't miss out on your next favorite book!

Join the Melange Books mailing list at
www.melange-books.com/mail.html

Death of a Philanderer
An original play by Peter J. McNab
©Peter J. McNab

Jaret: Tall, handsome. Leader personality, confident. A touch arrogant. Late twenties. Dresses well.

Detective Harry Rush: Trench coat. Rumpled suit. Hair sticking out. Harry Rush is the same actor as Jaret. Moves in an erratic fashion.

Nicholas: Average height. Nervous. Early twenties. Casual clothing, long baggy shirt. Nervous, lack of confidence.

Jon: Average height. Fifties. Good suit. The professor of the class. Feels superior to the students in his class.

Terri: Blonde, pretty woman. Early thirties. Giggles frequently. Short skirt, long blouse/top. Flirty.

Veronica, Ronnie: Tall. Sophisticated dresser. Thirties. Wearing a top with front buttons/zipper. Moves gracefully.

Karrie: Brunette, short hair, average height. Conservative dresser; pants, shirt. Late thirties. Strict looking woman; her sexual orientation is unknown. Aggressive personality.

Jaret, Harry Rush played by	Paul Church
Nicholas played by	Mitch Donnelly
Jon played by	Tyler Burgess
Terri played by	Brenda Thompson
Veronica played by	Tanya Conner
Kerri played by	Jessica Knowles
Stage Manager	Jessica Knowles
Director	Peter J. McNab

Set: Cocktail party in Terri's apartment. The audience sees the living room next to the kitchen. Overhead head lamps light the living room or kitchen according to where the scene is being played. Alternately, a rolling screen can be pulled in front of one room or the other.

The living room has a front door, a door to the bedroom, and the bathroom. The three doors are at the rear of the stage. There is an open entrance to the kitchen.

Furniture: The living room has a couch, chair, coffee table. The kitchen has a table, plus two chairs. Fake fridge, cupboards.

Our cast is milling around in the living room, drinking. On the coffee table we have food nibbles, plus a knife for cutting the cheese platter, sausage. Music is playing from a stereo.

JARET

(Walking confidently to the centre of the living room to Jon, who is standing by himself. Both are holding drinks.)

Well, Jon, this is a nice little party for our graduation class. I didn't expect our instructor would be here, but I guess you're part of the lottery group as well.

JON

(JON appraises Jaret briefly before replying, looking slightly annoyed.)

I hadn't realized we were on a first name basis. Yes, I'm here for the same reason you are. Terri, send us all of who contributed to the lottery fund an invite to receive our share of the winnings. I suppose she could have just sent out cheques, but she believed some of us would like to see each other one more time.

JARET

The lottery money does make it worthwhile to get together. I hadn't thought the course on the Logic of Psychology was worthy of getting together for a celebration.

(JARET smirks.)

No offence intended.

JON

Considering the source, none taken.

(JON turns to his side, welcoming at the approaching Terri.)
TERRI

(TERRI is grinning as she makes her way to Jon. She initially ignores Jaret, touching Jon on his arm.)
Mr. Stewart, it's so wonderful to see you again. I remember those lectures you gave me, I mean us. Your course was my favourite.
(TERRI finally acknowledges Jaret, frowning slightly as she speaks to him.)
Hello Jaret. I'm glad to see you as well.

JARET

Thank you, it was nice to receive your invite. You're looking very nice.
(JARET leans toward Terri, placing a hand on her shoulder briefly.)

TERRI
(TERRI giggles and tosses her hair.)

Thanks. Maybe it has something to do with the spa treatment I had yesterday. I feel good. I am so looking forward to seeing everyone from our Logic of Psychology classes. Mr. Stewart did such a great job of making sure everyone in the class joined in discussions and I feel I know everyone very well.
(JARET suddenly starts coughing as he is about to take a drink.)

JON

Please call me Jon. I believe I have some very good memories of that time as well.

TERRI

I don't see your wife here. Is she doing alright?

JON

Yes, she is doing okay, thank you for asking. She just didn't feel it was a social event she wanted to attend so I'm here by myself.

TERRI

That's too bad she couldn't make it.
(TERRI moves closer to Jon, putting a hand on his waist.)
Although I'm sure we can have a good time anyway.

JARET
(Looking at the ceiling momentarily.)

Yes, I'm quite certain good times will be had tonight. I think it is time for me to obtain another drink. I'll leave you two so you can ... converse.

(JARET walks away.)
JON

Terri, I must say I was very pleased at your personal invitation. I did imply to my wife that this going to a rather dry affair she wouldn't appreciate. I missed you after our class ended and I'm sorry circumstances prevented me from contacting you.

TERRI

It would have led to problems with us if we stayed in contact. I can't believe the police actually followed up on the stupid stalking charge and monitored you. That silly girl should be pleased you took an interest in her welfare and wanted to make sure she was safe.

(TERRI gives Jon a quick hug.)
JON

Thank you for your understanding. Perhaps we can go for a walk and catch up on a few things.

TERRI

I would like that.
(TERRI and JON exit off the stage via the front door. Jaret and Nichols move to front of the stage.)

JARET

Well, buddy, how's it going? I heard you have a job with the government.

NICHOLAS

Uh, yeah. It's a job. How about you, Jaret? How is your business going?

JARET

It's a land development corporation, so it has its ups and downs. Still, I do alright.
(JARET slaps Nicholas on the side of his shoulder. Nicholas jumps at the contact.)
Are you seeing anyone new? I remember you were really bummed out when Sherri dumped you.

NICOLAS

No, not much luck with women. I, I guess they don't see much in me.

JARET

Shit man, that's too bad. You know women are easy to get if you know a couple of tricks. Just gotta be confident. Take charge. Flash some money, even if you don't have much. Find an interesting hobby. Chicks dig odd stuff. What do you do besides work?

NICHOLAS

Uh, I hunt. I like being out in the woods by myself.

JARET

That won't get you a girl. Most think deer are too cute to shoot. Hey, I know Ronnie is single. Make a play for her.
(He nods his head toward Veronica as she approaches.)

VERONICA

(VERONICA walks slowly to join Jaret and Nicholas. She makes eye contact with both men before speaking)
Hello gentlemen. It is nice seeing you again.

JARET

Ronnie, wow, I have to say you look fantastic. Doesn't she, Nicholas.

NICHOLAS

Uh, yeah. Really pretty.

VERONICA

Actually, a few weeks ago I decided to go by my given name Veronica. I'm putting my winnings of the lottery money into my new clothing design company. Veronica Designs sounds better than Ronnie's Fashions.

(VERONICA smiles, clearly pleased at her status.)

Now, do tell me how you are two doing. Making use of Logic of Psychology course?

JARET
(Laughs.)

What a bullshit course. It was okay as far as the classroom discussions, but not something that works in the real world. I guess I can figure out people without relaying on some textbook or an instructor who chases skirts.

VERONICA
(Lightly punches Jaret on the shoulder. She laughs.)

What a horrible thing to say about Jon. It may be true, but still a terrible thing to say.

NICOLAS

I liked the course. It taught me something.

(He looks down at the floor.)
JARET
(Looks at his empty glass.)

Damn, must be a hole in the bottom of the glass. Anyone else for a refill?

VERONICA

Some more red wine, please.

(VERONICA hands Jaret her empty glass. The lights flitter off and then back on.)

Well, that would be interesting. A party in the dark.

NICOLAS

I heard they're doing construction work in the neighbourhood, and that there may be some interruptions in power. Could you get me another beer, Jaret?

(NICOLAS drains his can of beer and puts it on the coffee table. When Jaret leaves, he has to draw Veronica's attention as she scans the room.)

VERONICA

I'm sorry, did you say something?

NICOLAS

Yes. I was wondering if you'd like to go out for drink, or even a coffee, sometime.

VERONICA

Oh, well, perhaps sometime we could. I'm really busy lately, so I'm not sure when we can get together.

(JARET returns with a can of beer, his own drink, but an empty wine glass.)

Where's my wine? Did you drink it carrying over here?

(VERONICA laughs)
JARET

The bottle was empty. What else would you like to have?

(JARET hands Nicolas his beer.)
VERONICA

I believe there's more wine in the kitchen. I'll take a look.

(VERONICA walks to the kitchen.)
JARET
(JARET watches her walk with interest.)

I should go and help her.

(JARET follows her to the kitchen.)
NICOLAS

(NICOLAS crosses his arms, looking upset as he watches Jaret enter the kitchen. The front door opens, drawing his attention. Jon, Terri and Karrie enter.)

TERRI

Look who we found walking down street looking lost.

(TERRI giggles as she tugs on Karrie's arm.)
KARRIE

I wasn't lost. I just had to park so damn far away.
(KARRIE picks up a can of beer, opens it and takes a long drink.)
That tastes good.

NICOLAS

Hi Karrie. It's good to see you.

KARRIE

(KARRIE appraises him as she walks over to where he's standing.)

Well, cowboy, it's good seeing you too.
(KARRIE taps her can of beer against his.)
Cheers.

NICOLAS

Cheers.
(NICOLAS is surprised by her friendliness toward him. He takes a quick gulp of his beer.)

TERRI

Why don't you two get reacquainted? I want to show Jon some of my lecture notes. I have a question about something.
(TERRI goes to the bedroom with Jon right behind her.)

KARRIE

You know, I was hoping we would be able to get together sometime.
(KARRIE grabs his shirt in one hand, pulling him closer to her.)
I think Terri is right, and we should get acquainted.

(KARRIE kisses Nicolas.)

NICOLAS
(NICOLAS drops his beer can. He kisses Karrie back.)

KARRIE

Come on, cowboy. Let's make use of our alone time here.
(KARRIE pushes Nicolas toward the couch where he falls on his back with her sitting on top of him. She manages to place her beer on the coffee table. She presses down on his shoulders, kissing him.

SCENE CHANGE: The overhead lamps in the living room are cut, and the lamps on the kitchen are turned on.)

VERONICA

See, I know where the wine is kept.
(VERONICA holds a bottle of wine as she stands by the counter.)

JARET

A smart girl like you likely knows a lot of things.
(JARET moves up close to her and puts his arm around her waist. He leans forward.)

VERONICA

Now I have to ask, are you going to start something you can't finish? Because I'm not the type of woman that likes to be played with. Are you the teasing type?

JARET

(JARET kisses her. She places the wine bottle on the counter, and she wraps her arms around his neck. They kiss, break apart, and kiss again. Jaret begins to kiss her neck, working downward. Veronica leans back, her hands sliding down his arms. Suddenly he pulls open her blouse (buttons fly, or zipper is pulled down. Veronica is wearing a lacy bra/bustier.)

VERONICA

Oh! You're such a bad boy.

JARET

But you like it.
(JARET directs her toward the table. He lifts her up and places her on the table. He climbs on top of the table as well, placing his body between her legs. OVERHEAD LAMPS go out in the kitchen. OVERHEAD LAMPS in the living room go on.)

KARRIE

You just relax, I'll take care of you.
(KARRIE is still on top of Nicolas on the couch. Suddenly a crash is heard from the kitchen. Karrie and Nicolas jump up from the couch. Karrie is still dressed, but her shirt is untucked. Nicolas is bare chested, his shirt on the floor. His pants are undone, barely staying up on his hips. His belt, also open, is weighed down by a closed knife in a leather holster. Karrie heads to the kitchen, with Nicolas close behind trying to hold up his pants. Terri and Jon emerge from the bedroom. Jon is missing his sports jacket, his shirt having some buttons undone. Terri is missing her skirt. Her blouse is long enough to cover her hips. Jon, Terri, Nicolas and Karrie all arrive at the kitchen. OVERHEAD LAMPS in the kitchen go on. In the kitchen, we see the table is turned over on its side. Slowly, Veronica and Jaret stand up from behind it.)

TERRI

What happened here? Is everyone alright?

JARET

Yes, we just kind of slipped and the table fell over. Sorry about the noise.
(JARET lifts the table back on its legs. Veronica pulls her open top closed but doesn't appear to be embarrassed.)

KARRIE

Hello Ronnie, Jaret. It's nice to see you.
(KARRIE walks over, giving Veronica a hug first and then Jaret.)

VERONICA

You can call me Veronica. I sort of did a name upgrade. You're looking nice. I think I've only seen you in blue jeans before.

(The lights flicker off for a few seconds before turning back on.)

TERRI

Darn power. I suggest we go back to the living room and resume our party. There's drink and food.

(TERRI looks at Nicolas.)

I think your pants are about to fall down.

NICOLAS

(NICOLAS suddenly realizes his exposure and pulls his pants up higher and does up his belt.)
I better get my shirt on.
(Nicolas hurries back to the living room. He quickly puts on his shirt and does up his pants. Terri and Jon follow. They sit on the couch holding hands and exchange a long kiss. Terri is still without her skirt. Nicolas standing by the coffee table. Terri uses a knife to cut a portion of cheese. She passes the knife to Jon, who after using it, gives it to Nicolas. They munch on food, looking toward the kitchen.)

NICOLAS

I wonder what they're doing in there.
(Karrie, Veronica and Jaret emerge from the kitchen. Jaret is between the two women, with arm around each. All three are laughing. Veronica's shirt is open as she places the wine bottle and a cork screw opener on the table. They stand around the coffee table near Nicolas. Jon and Terri stand and move to the rest, forming a circle.)

VERONICA

Could someone open the wine bottle? I have trouble using these openers.

JON

I'll do it. It's something a gentleman should do for a lady.
(JON gives Jaret a stare as he picks up the opener -server's style of opener and opens the knife portion to cut off the plastic film covering the top of the wine bottle.)

TERRI
(She starts to dance to a song playing.)

Oh, I love this song.

JARET

It's a great dance piece.
(JARET takes her hand and begins to dance with her. She wraps along their arms and they end up face to face with each other. He places his other arm behind her and bends her backward, leaning into her. He pulls her back to an upright position and they dance for a few more seconds before stopping.
(Jon has opened the wine bottle and filled a wine glass for Veronica.)

TERRI

(Smiling at him.)
My, you're such a good dancer.

JARET

Perhaps we can go dancing sometime.

(JARET leers at her, raising his eyebrows.)

TERRI

That would be fun. Now, I would like to propose a toast to former classmates that have become friends and also to celebrate our lottery winnings. It isn't big enough to retire on but will allow everyone to buy something special.

(TERRI picks up an envelope from the coffee table, taking out several cheques. She looks at the first cheque.)

Jaret, here's your cheque. What do you plan to do with your winnings?

JARET

Invest in some land holdings. Double my money in five years. If anyone wants to get on the action, let me know.

(TERRI hands the next cheque to Jon, repeating her question she asked Jaret.)

JON

It is not a large sum. Perhaps I'll take an extended vacation in Europe. I most certainly won't invest in any dubious land holdings venture.

(KARRIE receives her cheque.)
KARRIE

I think I'll buy a nice crossbow. I do like hunting.

(Karrie nudges Nicolas.)

Fancy going on a hunt for deer sometime?

(The lights flicker, and then go out. Moments later someone moans and the sound of someone falling to the floor. The lights go back on. Jaret is lying on the floor, blood seeping out of his chest as he lies on his back.)

Terri screams, followed by Veronica and then Karrie, each at a different pitch.

END OF SCENE ONE
SCENE TWO

(Everyone is standing around a body (pillows) covered by a blanket. The body is next to the coffee table. One or two guests continue to nibble at the food. The door bell rings and Terri hurries over to open it to the detective, Harry Rush.)

TERRI

Thank God, you're here. Something terrible has happened. One of our guests has died.

HARRY

Have no worries, my dear. Detective Harry Rush is here to discover what has transpired.
(Harry strides into room. He looks around, peering into the kitchen and the bedroom. He finally points at the body.)
Is this the body?

TERRI

Good guess. Yes, poor Jaret was stabbed in the chest.

HARRY

(HARRY lifts up part of the blanket and peers at the body. He shakes his head and a few seconds pass before he speaks.)
Yes, I can confirm that's a body alright. Stabbed in the heart. Blood all over his shirt. Nasty bit of stuff.
(HARRY drops the blanket back over the body.)
Damn good looking guy though. Now who did it?

TERRI

Isn't that why you're here, to find who did it?

HARRY

Well, yes. But it never hurts to ask first. It would save a lot of trouble if the perpetrator would just confess. Now who saw what happened?

VERONICA

No one. The lights went out and someone took the opportunity to murder Jaret. This is all so terrible.

(VERONICA begins to cry. Nicolas tries to put his arm around her but she quickly moves away from him.)

HARRY

So, no witnesses. I'll have to use my amazing sleuthing skills.

(HARRY suddenly points a finger at Veronica, snapping out a question.)

Did you kill Jaret in a fit of rage?

VERONICA

What?! Of course not. We always liked each other. If fact after the party tonight, we were going to his place to spend the night. Why would I murder a man I was going to have sex with? Maybe afterward, depending if he failed to remember my name.

HARRY

Good point, although I have to wonder if you get many second dates.

(HARRY looks at Jon.)

How about you sir? What are your feelings toward Jaret? Were you two secretly lovers?

JON

Are you an imbecile? He was a student in my class. That's it. He was smart, arrogant and always chasing women. At least in my classroom. I'm also a married man, who certainly would not have any interest in someone like Jaret.

KARRIE

Yes, but we do know how some other students that were of interest to you.
(KARRIE looks at Terri.)

TERRI
(TERRI shrugs and smiles.)

I like older men. I find them so sophisticated and sexy.

HARRY

Oh, really?
(HARRY straightens his tie and smooths down his trench coat.)
How about you, Nicholas? What was your relationship with the deceased?

NICOLAS

(Acting nervous, his fingers working against each other.)
Uh, we were just friends. I had a couple of beers with him a couple of times. We got along okay. I didn't kill him.

HARRY

Aha! That's exactly what a murderer would say, claiming they didn't kill anyone.
(He holds up a finger for emphasis.)

KARRIE

What would someone innocent say? Claim they did kill someone?
(KARRIE crosses her arms and looks up at the ceiling.)

HARRY

Please keep your opinions to yourself. This is a serious murder investigation. This murder will be solved by a well trained, experienced detective who will carefully analyse all clues.

KARRIE

And yet we have you to solve the case.

HARRY

I'll take that as a compliment. Now, madam, what are your feelings toward our victim?

KARRIE

I thought he was a hunk. I was going to his place after the party tonight. I certainly didn't have a reason to kill him.

HARRY

I thought Veronica was going to his place after the party.

KARRIE

Yeah, it was going to be a threesome. I suppose Veronica and I will have to figure out a different place now.
(KARRIE walks over to Veronica. She gives her a hug and they exchange a quick kiss.)

HARRY

Doesn't anyone hate this man? How about you, Terri? What was your relationship with him?

TERRI

I thought he was cute. We had sex a few times. And he was a very good dancer.

HARRY

I thought you went out with Jon?

TERRI

I did. Also with Jaret. Also with... Let's just say I'm a people person.

HARRY

This is all very interesting, but one of you did murder this poor, handsome fella.
(HARRY starts to nibble from the food platter on the coffee table. After a couple of bites, he picks up the knife to cut a slice of cheese.)

KARRIE

What are you doing?! Isn't that the knife used to stab Jaret?

HARRY

(HARRY is startled and juggles the knife. After a few seconds, it tumbles to the floor. Harry jumps back, staring at the knife.)
Stabbed with this knife? Why am I the last to know how he was killed?
(HARRY shakes his head and holds his arms in the air, clearly annoyed at the lack of information.)
Well, this actually helps a lot.

JON

How? By touching the knife you've put your own fingerprints on it over the killer's.

HARRY

Your comment is something someone might make less skilled in detective work. However, this knife was not the weapon used to commit murder.

(HARRY picks up the knife, waving it around for emphasis. Everyone else steps away from Harry.)

You see, there isn't any blood on this knife. Therefore, it was not used to kill our victim. That means the real knife used in this hideous crime is still here.

TERRI

So, where is it?

HARRY

Ah, that is the question. Where indeed? Or more accurately, who has it?

(Harry points at Jon.)

You sir. I need to search you for a knife.

(JON steps up to Harry. As he holds his arms out to his sides, Harry pats him down awkwardly.)

Alright, you're clear. Next.

(HARRY beckons Veronica to come forward. She walks up to him and puts her hands on her hips.)

VERONICA

Search away. I really don't have many places to hide a weapon.

(Veronica smiles, looking amused as Harry pulls apart her top tentatively- still unbuttoned from her encounter in the kitchen- one side at a time. He gently pats her back and her sides. Harry lifts up her skirt by the hem at least a few inches. He stands.)

HARRY

You seem to be free of any weapon as well. Perhaps Miss. Karrie will be next.

KARRIE

Okay, but you be damn careful where you put your hands, or there might be a double homicide.

(She stands in front of Harry, crossing her arms.)
HARRY

I am a professional. Have no worries. I do not see you as a beautiful woman, but merely a suspect.

KARRIE

Are you saying I'm not beautiful? Are you looking for a good smack?

(KARRIE raises her voice, sounding angry.)
HARRY

No, no, no. You are very beautiful. I just meant you can trust me.

(He nervously pats her.)
KARRIE

I don't trust any man. Are you quite done touching me?

HARRY

Yes, I didn't feel anything unusual.

KARRIE

I should hope not, depending on exactly what you were searching for.

TERRI

I suppose you can check me out next.
(TERRI doesn't act apprehensive as she approaches Harry. She stands with her back to the audience and places her hands behind her head. She is still without her skirt. Harry pats her over her blouse, lifting up the edge of her top very carefully.)
Do you want me to take off my shirt? You'll see I'm literally not hiding anything.

HARRY

No, please, that won't be necessary. I can see you don't have a hidden knife. That leaves Mr. Nicolas. Sir, I need to check your person for a knife.
(NICOLAS moves slowly toward Harry. Suddenly he pulls out his hunting knife. He holds the knife in a threatening manner at the group. Harry jumps into a martial arts defensive posture.)
Drop that knife! I'm a trained professional.

NICOLAS

Keep back! I'll use this knife on anyone who gets close.

VERONICA

Why did you kill Jaret? I thought you were friends.

NICOLAS

Friends? He told me I should go after you and then he makes out with you in the kitchen. Karrie goes from me on the couch to planning a threesome with Jaret. He gets two women and I get none. How is that fair? Even Terri would rather be with that old goat of a professor than me. How does he rate higher than me? But I didn't kill him.

(NICOLAS continues to be increasingly agitated. He points the knife at each person as he makes his speech. Harry slowly moves behind Nicolas, waiting for an opportunity to disarm him.)

TERRI

(TERRI notices Harry sneaking closer to Nicolas, deciding to help to distract him.)

"Hey, Nicholas. I always thought you were kind of cute. If you had only asked me out, you could have had this.

(TERRI lifts/opens her top, flashing Nicolas. Terri still has her back to the audience. Nicolas acts surprise. His jaw drops, and so does the knife from his grasp. Harry quickly jumps in and wrestles him to the floor, where he handcuffs him. He pulls Nicolas to his feet. Terri closes/pulls down her top.)

HARRY

So, you thought you could get away with murder but failed to take in account the great Harry Rush would be the one investigating the crime.

NICOLAS

But I didn't do it. I didn't kill Jaret.

HARRY

Ha! A likely story. No one else has a knife here. This is your knife. Therefore, you must be guilty.

(HARRY pulls a pink handkerchief from his pocket to pick up the knife.)

KARRIE

I have two questions. If that was the knife used to kill Jaret, then why isn't there any blood on it? And why do you have a pink handkerchief?

HARRY

(HARRY examines the knife closely. He sighs and looks up at the ceiling.)
There isn't any blood on this knife, so it wasn't the murder weapon. Damn it, this is most inconvenient not having a murder weapon to examine. I suppose this means Nicolas didn't do it.

NICOLAS

I told you so. Will you take off these cuffs now?

HARRY

I might as well.

(HARRY removes the cuffs from Nicolas)
KARRIE

You still didn't answer why your handkerchief is pink.

HARRY

I washed my whites with red pyjamas.

KARRIE

That certainly leads to another question. Red pyjamas?

217

HARRY

I'll be doing investigating and questions here, thank you very much.
(HARRY begins to pace around the living room. He again peers into the kitchen and acts like he's searching for clues.)
Jaret was murdered with a sharp object, such as a knife. We have found two knifes without blood on them, thus they were not a murder weapon. Therefore, there must be another knife that has not be accounted for. None of you suspects has a weapon hidden on your person. Where could that murder weapon be hidden?

VERONICA

If we're depending on you to solve this case, it may be a very long night.
(VERONICA pours herself a glass of wine. The bottle and wine glass are on the coffee table. She takes a sip.)
Nice wine.
(She picks up the wine bottle, examining the label.)

JON

Yes, it is Bordeaux. A lovely French wine. It is, of course, a blend. This particular one is dominated by Cabernet Sauvignon.

TERRI

It must be a good wine, because it uses a real cork. Not one of those cheap plastic ones.

(TERRI picks up the cork.)
HARRY

A cork? So where is the opener?
(He begins to look around for the opener, checking the coffee table, then surrounding area. Then he returns to the coffee table, moving items

around. He picks up the cheese tray, revealing the cork screw. He uses his handkerchief to pick up the corkscrew with blood on the knife portion.)

Aha! The murder weapon. Who does this belong too?

TERRI

It's mine, but I didn't use it.

(TERRI points a finger at Jon.)

He did.

JON

Don't women have any loyalty?

HARRY

Why did you do it?

(HARRY handcuffs Jon)
JON

That punk never showed me any respect. Then he has the gull to make a move on my girlfriend, Terri. I suddenly saw an opportunity to teach him a lesson and I took it. I'll bet he's sorry he crossed me now.

HARRY

I doubt he's sorry for anything now. You, sir, are charged with murder and adultery.

JON

Adultery isn't a crime.

HARRY

Tell that to your wife.

(He leads Jon to the front door.)

Another case solved by the great detective Harry Rush.

TERRI

What about the body? Are you just going to leave it here?

Harry

No worries. It won't move by itself. I'll have the body picked up soon. I just have to fill out the required forms.

(Harry exits with Jon.)
VERONICA

I don't know about the rest of you, but I for one don't like to party around a dead body. Unless it's Halloween, of course.

KARRIE

You and I can go to my place. No dead bodies there.

VERONICA

Sounds good to me.
(She takes Karrie by the hand and heads to the front door.)
Thanks for the party, Terri. Next time at my place.
(Karrie and Veronica wave goodbye and exit.)

TERRI

Well, Nicolas, that just leaves you, me and a dead body. I'd rather not continue our party around a body.

(She walks over to the bedroom.)

NICOLAS

The bedroom would be a better place to continue our party.

TERRI

You and me in the bedroom together? No, no, no. I'm going to put some more clothes on. You wait outside here and then we'll go for a pizza.

(She enters the bedroom and closes the door.)

NICOLAS

(He looks disappointed but directs his comments to the Jaret's body.)

Well, Jaret, I guess we were drinking buddies. But doesn't mean we were friends. You used me to make yourself look good. Now I'm looking much better than you, or at least to women who prefer guys who are still breathing.

(Terri, now wearing a skirt, exits the bedroom. She takes Nicolas' arm and they leave via the front door.)

JARET

(The lights are turned off for a moment, then the lights in the kitchen go on. We see Jaret standing by the table drinking a glass of wine. Jaret has a dusting of white powder on his face and other exposed skin. White latex gloves can be used to give his hands a pale appearance. He turns and faces the audience.)

Don't be alarmed. I'm quite dead, and not the zombie kind of dead either. I'm just a ghost. A ghost that can drink wine may seem unusual, but I assure you there are stranger things in this world than that.

(The rest of the cast walk into the kitchen, standing around Jaret as he concludes his speech.)

It has been said, All the world is a stage, and men and women are merely players. If that is true, then the players on this stage wish to thank this audience for coming to our play and we hope you enjoyed Death of a Philander.

(The cast joins hands and bow to the audience)

END OF PLAY

THANK YOU FOR READING

Did you enjoy this book?

We invite you to leave a review at the website of your choice, such as Goodreads, Amazon, Barnes & Noble, etc.

DID YOU KNOW THAT LEAVING A REVIEW...

- Helps other readers find books they may enjoy.
- Gives you a chance to let your voice be heard.
- Gives authors recognition for their hard work.
- Doesn't have to be long. A sentence or two about why you liked the book will do.

ABOUT THE AUTHOR

J. H. (Jack) Wear lives in Edmonton, Alberta with his wife, Lorrie. They have three sons, and two grandsons. Logic notwithstanding, Lorrie blames Jack for the lack of females in the family.

Jack took up writing later than most authors. After finishing a career with Xerox, he soon felt bored and started selling beverages as a liquor agent. Over several glasses of Sauvignon Blanc, he wrote his first novel, submitted it and suddenly became a published author. This astonished everyone, especially every English teacher he had in school.

He continued with writing, adding a trilogy, along with several short stories. Most of his writing is in the fantasy and science fiction genres, although his latest novel is a murder mystery.

His current projects are a science fiction novel, a murder mystery and trying to convince his single sons their mother needs a granddaughter.

www.jhwear.com

ALSO BY JACK WEAR

A Taste of Murder

Witches and Warriors

Dragons in the Water

A Hole in the Universe (Available in 2020)